BLACK MAGIC

As the beautiful dancer came closer, the other guests jostled her, but she only slid sinuously past, her arms making a graceful arch in the air as if she heard an inner music.

Sir Richard clutched his wine glass hard, barely aware of the crush of people around him, everyone babbling, laughing, and flirting. He only saw the onyx gaze so firmly trained on him behind the sequined mask of the gypsy.

Her white peasant blouse revealed most of her creamy shoulders and her full ruffled silk skirt shimmered with as many hues as the veil around her head. A slim ankle flashed as she swirled, and then she came to a stop right in front of him.

He had recognized her, of course. No other lady present had such a magnificent black mane, or so provocative a smile. She was taller than the others as well.

"Miss Ashcroft, I presume."

BOOK YOUR PLACE ON OUR WEBSITE AND MAKE THE READING CONNECTION!

We've created a customized website just for our very special readers, where you can get the inside scoop on everything that's going on with Zebra, Pinnacle and Kensington books.

When you come online, you'll have the exciting opportunity to:

- View covers of upcoming books
- Read sample chapters
- Learn about our future publishing schedule (listed by publication month *and author*)
- Find out when your favorite authors will be visiting a city near you
- Search for and order backlist books from our online catalog
- Check out author bios and background information
- Send e-mail to your favorite authors
- Meet the Kensington staff online
- Join us in weekly chats with authors, readers and other guests
- Get writing guidelines
- AND MUCH MORE!

Visit our website at
http://www.kensingtonbooks.com

THE ASHCROFT CURSE

Maria Greene

ZEBRA BOOKS
Kensington Publishing Corp.
http://www.kensingtonbooks.com

ZEBRA BOOKS are published by

Kensington Publishing Corp.
850 Third Avenue
New York, NY 10022

All Kensington titles, imprints and distributed lines are available at special quantity discounts for bulk purchases for sales promotion, premiums, fund-raising, educational or institutional use.

Special book excerpts or customized printings can also be created to fit specific needs. For details, write or phone the office of the Kensington Special Sales Manager: Kensington Publishing Corp., 850 Third Avenue, New York, NY 10022. Attn. Special Sales Department. Phone: 1-800-221-2647.

Zebra and the Z logo Reg. U.S. Pat. & TM Off.

First Printing: April 2003
10 9 8 7 6 5 4 3 2 1

Printed in the United States of America

One

There was no doubt that the curse existed. Disbelievers would believe after reading this evidence and listening to her tale. Jillian Ashcroft looked up from the frayed and brittle, yellowed letter in her lap. She had carefully handled the one-hundred-and-fifty year old paper, and she wondered how much more it could stand without crumbling altogether. She had read it many times in hope of finding some clue to an ancient hoax, some evidence of an ill-chosen jest, but had found none.

Long, long ago, at the time of her great-great-great-grandfather, a witch, a living, breathing witch, had put a curse on the Ashcrofts. Who could believe that such creatures existed? But they did, at least back then. She had the proof right here in her hands.

Jillian inhaled sharply, holding her breath as she remembered the tales of violent deaths among her forefathers, drownings at sea, sudden deadly strikes of lightning, inexplicable storms over Lindenwood, her ancestral home in Devon. All because of an ancient wrongdoing one of her ancestors perpetrated against the Endicott family in the neighboring Cornwall.

More often than not, Jill had both feet on the ground and a healthy skepticism toward anything that

concerned the supernatural, yet . . . she couldn't deny
there was evidence as plain as a pikestaff for those
who looked. And she had looked, as she desired to
put an end to the Ashcroft curse.

A rather large portion of the wild Ashcroft blood
undoubtedly flowed in her veins. She could count pirates and mercenaries among her ancestors, and
there had been long-ago connections to the Orient
and the countries around the Mediterranean. Her
black hair, dark and slightly slanted eyes, and golden
skin, were those forebears' legacy to her. The
Ashcrofts had been an inventive and prosperous lot—
before the curse. Now the estate only scraped by.
Thank God, she'd inherited considerable funds from
her mother.

A knock on the door startled her out of her reverie.
She smoothed her unruly hair, which still hadn't been
put up into its customary chignon, and adjusted her
simple yellow morning gown of twilled silk. After setting the letter carefully aside on the nightstand, she
called out, "Please enter."

Her chaperone, the rotund Lady Honoria Iddings,
Aunt Iddy, who was the youngest daughter of an earl,
a spinster of middle years, a lover of chocolate confits,
and the deceased Mrs. Ashcroft's youngest sister,
stepped inside. She fumbled nearsightedly along the
silk-paneled wall to the nearest armchair where she
sat down with a moan.

"I don't believe I've ever lived through such a heat
wave," she said, fanning herself vigorously with a white
handkerchief. "It's the outside of enough."

She stared at Jill, but Jill knew she couldn't see anything but vague outlines. Aunt Iddy was too vain to wear
eyeglasses all the time, and Jill—though she granted it
was wicked of her—was delighted with the modicum of

freedom Aunt Iddy's myopia gave her. Jill could have kissed every gentleman at the house party without her aunt being any wiser. Such liberty could not be anything but gratifying. Not that she lured young bucks behind curtains for bouts of illicit kissing, but the array of possibilities gave her an anticipatory thrill.

"What are you doing, Jill? I thought you would join the picnic. A party is gathering downstairs."

Jill glanced out to the tall open window, and was acutely aware of the oppressive atmosphere over the Sussex Downs. Mint-green silk curtains fluttered in the rising wind. "No, Aunt Iddy. I think it will rain within the hour. I have no desire to get my feet wet."

"Hmph! You sound very sure of yourself. When did you acquire the skill of divining the weather?"

Jill laughed. "If you wore your spectacles you would be able to see the bank of gray clouds moving over the horizon even as we speak."

"Don't be saucy." Aunt Iddy sighed and tapped her fingertips on the armrest. "How will you find an admirer if you stay cloistered in your bedchamber all day? You should join the other guests and vigorously exercise your scintillating conversation and considerable charm."

Jill laughed. "Don't fly into one of your pets, Aunt Iddy. I'll find an admirer soon enough. That's why we're here, after all, husband hunting." She shuddered inwardly. "But first, there's the small matter of the Ashcroft curse. I've been plotting."

Aunt Iddy emitted a wail. "I don't understand why you insisted coming down to Sussex and to this house party when all you talk about is Lindenwood and the dratted curse."

"This visit is all part of the plan to destroy the curse."

"If I didn't know you so well, Jill, I would be convinced you have windmills in your head. I suspect some of the other guests think you do. I've noticed that they move out of the room when you enter." Aunt Iddy heaved a third sigh. "Speaking about family curses in public is no way to attract an admirer, and you'd better find one soon, before you're left on the shelf."

"You don't seem to have suffered on the shelf, Auntie," Jill replied baldly. "Such freedom you've enjoyed."

Aunt Iddy snorted in outrage. "You're speaking like a veritable thimblewit, and not like the lady I know you to be. If your mother were alive, she would surely shrivel in humiliation at such unbefitting speech. She worked very hard at making a proper lady out of you. And she would have wished for a suitable marriage."

Jill laughed and whirled around until the ends of her white sash swept outward. "I am a lady. Can you find any fault with my appearance other than my hair? Jane hasn't had time to fix it yet."

"You're too high-spirited by far, and this talk about ancient curses will surely send the gentlemen scurrying into hiding."

"Someone like Father wouldn't scurry. He knew everything there was to know about magic and old witches' brews. And the stars. He cured all kinds of ills. He knew much more about healing than did the physician in the village."

"You're right there, but your father was a bit peculiar. It seems that the curse didn't touch him though, as he died in a common coaching accident. There's nothing strange or superstitious about that."

"The coachman swore he saw a horse, as wild and black as the darkest night, frightening the team until they plunged into a ditch. Ever since that day, the servants have said that Father died because of the curse, and they are right." Jill dared her chaperone to contradict her.

"It saddens me no end to hear you talk like that, Jill. You are damned with the curse yourself. You have nothing else on your mind, and if you don't stop speculating about it, you'll step into some pond without even noticing it, and drown."

"I'm not as dim-witted or scatter-brained as that," Jill said airily. She folded the letter carefully and placed it in her father's yellowed diary. She'd read his journal so many times she could remember every single word. "I've told you, Aunt Iddy, that I've found the way to break the curse. Tonight at the ball, I shall put my plan into motion, and before you know it, Lindenwood and the Ashcrofts will be free." She sighed. "Not that I want Alvin Ashcroft to get my childhood home, but I have no choice."

"The estate was entailed to him, and there's nothing you can do to break the entail." Aunt Iddy rested her flapping handkerchief in her lap. "He's been slavering like a mad dog after you this spring. He would like to marry you. Think of it, Lindenwood would forever be your home if you agreed to the union."

"Cousin Alvin has been slavering after my money, not me. You know he has pockets to let, and the expensive upkeep of Lindenwood will ruin him. I don't want to give him the fortune I inherited from Mama, but I'd hate to see Lindenwood fall into disrepair."

"He not only wants your funds, but he wants *you,* Jillian."

Jill set her jaw. "He shan't have me. Alvin is not trustworthy. He's greedy and selfish, the worst combination of character traits."

"Who isn't selfish?" Aunt Iddy said with much feeling. "I have yet to meet a gentleman who doesn't put his horses or his stomach before his wife or fiancée. Yet we cannot live without the vexatious creatures." She sent her charge a myopic glance. "If Alvin is so terrible, who do you consider worthy of your love?"

"No one—at the moment. I have yet to find a gentleman who is kind and understanding and patient, who has great humor, and who will listen to me, to me, not just brush me off as an inferior kind of species just because I'm female."

"Someone you can lead by the nose then," Aunt Iddy commented sarcastically. "Or a saint." She chuckled. "Such a man doesn't exist, and if he did, he wouldn't be looking in your direction. Saints don't hold with witches and old curses."

Jill gave a rueful laugh. "Then I shall remain on the shelf. There's no use trying to dissuade me from my path, dearest Aunt Iddy."

"Bolting horses could not dislodge you from your disastrous path," the older lady said with another sigh. "I might be a crotchety old fidget, but you're too stubborn for your own good. Young ladies are supposed to be soft and pliable, not like a . . . a—"

"Why don't you say the word, Auntie?"

Aunt Iddy looked suspiciously innocent. "What word, pray?"

"She-devil, mayhap? Or hoyden?"

Aunt Iddy clutched her handkerchief to her plump chest. "Oooh, Jill, I didn't say that!"

"But that's what you're thinking, and all the other guests as well. And all just because Father studied things one can't see with the naked eye."

Aunt Iddy cringed visibly, and Jill felt a stab of disappointment. Was she such a freak because she wanted to dispel the curse that hung over her family? Surely she had the right to live a long peaceful life without worrying if she was going to be the next Ashcroft victim of misfortune.

"You're just like your father. You have an uncanny knack for reading people's thoughts, Jill. It's not seemly, and it gives me quite a fright at times."

"Nonsense. That's pure coincidence. I can't read your thoughts, or anyone else's, but I can sense a falsehood a furlong away, and I abhor shifty people."

"That's as may be, but no one is perfect, and you must learn to be more tolerant." Aunt Iddy rose and moved across the floor to enfold Jill in a maternal embrace. "Oh, Jill, I wish you nothing but happiness. If only you were more biddable, not so outspoken and full of mischief. I would have an easier time of it."

Jill softened inside, and smelled the scent of roses that her chaperone always wore. She would forever have a fond memory of that scent even if her path separated from that of Aunt Iddy in the future. She could recall that fragrance more easily than the faint floral scent her mother had used. Most fondly of all, she recalled the aroma of her father's "medicine" room, which had been filled with drying herbs and mosses of all kinds. She missed him. He'd been dead two years—he died ten years after Mrs. Ashcroft.

When Jill had come out of mourning for her father, Alvin Ashcroft had done everything to ingratiate himself with her.

Aunt Iddy was doing her outmost to introduce Jill to every well-fixed bachelor in London. The season had been hectic, and here they were, houseguests at Lord Celtborn's vast estate in East Sussex, in the lap of the South Downs, not far from the coast.

As yet she had no particular admirers, but that didn't daunt Jill. She knew the reputation of the Ashcrofts, especially that of her father, had preceded her to London from Devon. It was understandable that no gentleman in his right mind would marry a potential witch. Not that she was one, of course, but some might believe that.

Jill knew of a man who could help her break the curse of the Ashcrofts—if she could persuade him. He would be at the ball tonight.

Jill pulled a box of chocolate bonbons from the drawer of her nightstand and offered it to her aunt.

"Here, dear Aunt Iddy, I'm frightfully sorry for all the trouble I've put you through this season. But tonight will be the beginning of the end, I promise."

The rain arrived and she felt as if it were bringing with it a new beginning.

Sir Richard Blackwood, who had reluctantly agreed to attend the ball at Celtborn's mansion, had arrived early. He stood on the wide terrace watching the rain pour, then move away. Beside him rested his old friend and host, Jerry, the Marquess of Celtborn, in a chair. Not only were they friends, but also neighbors. Richard was as fond of Jerry as if they were brothers, and hoped that Jerry's chatter could cheer him up.

Today had been a difficult day, hours of tallying the estate accounts with his steward, and the dashed funds hadn't come close to covering the costs. He wished he could forget his financial problems for one night. . . .

And talking to Jerry dulled the hollow grief in his chest and soothed the raw edges of his loss, feelings that still lingered. His darling sister was dead, and no crying or begging would ever bring her back. "Your park is even more spectacular this year, Jerry," he said and pointed at the profusion of roses in the borders. "You've outdone yourself."

"I take great interest in growing things, you know that." The plump Lord Celtborn turned to Sir Richard with a good-natured smile. "You haven't put in those ponds at Eversley as I told you. You could stock some trout."

"You well know I can barely afford the upkeep of the main buildings, let alone make major changes to the park." Sir Richard sipped the port that Jerry had offered as he arrived. "It's difficult enough to pay the gardener. Don't want to send the fellow off. He's worked at Eversley forty years."

"Well, your problems will soon be over once you marry Laura Endicott. Even if she is a bit odd in her desire for seclusion, she has a large fortune." He stood and stared at his friend narrowly. "You don't seem too thrilled at the prospect of marriage."

Sir Richard frowned. "Father made me offer for Laura before he died, but it seems so long ago now. Some balderdash of doing an old friend a favor, and I felt that Laura would probably make as good a wife as any of the dashing London ladies. Father was Laura's godfather, you see, and he was concerned about her fate. As far as I know, she lives alone with only the servants and an ancient aunt for company."

"Perhaps it was old Blackwood's way of providing for your future when he suggested that Laura needed your protection. No need mention the touchy word 'money.' Nevertheless her funds will come in handy."

"I'd rather not sell my freedom for money. There must be other ways to solve my problems. I'm looking into the newest ways to increase crops and I see great

opportunity for profit there. Yet, I'm formally court-
ing Laura now, and she accepted our union—"

Jerry laughed and patted his friend on the shoulder. "With your devilish dark-eyed charm, you could
have any female you desire. Dammit, Blackwood, you
ought to marry for love, like I did. I don't see how you
could be so stuffy as to offer for the chit by mail all
those years ago."

"Father handled it."

"Love is still the key to a successful marriage."

"Love? All my energy goes into solving the problems of Eversley. I don't have time for romantic
dalliance, and Miss Laura Endicott agreed to marry
me without flowery speeches." He set the crystal glass
down with a click on the marble balustrade. "Besides,
Laura knows all about me. Her father evidently prepared her well for the possibility of an alliance
between the Blackwoods and the Endicotts."

"You're much too rigid and precise, old boy, always
thinking about dull things like crops and estate man-
agement. You didn't used to be like that at Oxford.
You were as wild and carefree as any of the young
bloods there. I must say the burden of Eversley has
changed you in an unpleasant way."

Richard stared at his friend, the merry blue eyes,
the round face, the thinning hair. If anyone other
than Jerry had spoken so boldly, Richard would've
called him out. The sudden flare of anger in his chest
died down. "I know you mean well, Jerry, but frankly,
my love life is none of your business."

"How can it be, when you don't have one?" Jerry
pointed out. "You've turned into a sour-faced recluse
at that boggy estate of yours. The sacrifice isn't worth
it. You can't rebuild your home with your bare hands.
It takes time and barrels of the ready."

"I can do it!" Sir Richard said, clenching his jaw in determination. "I will drain and cultivate those bogs if it's the last thing I do!"

Jerry raised his hands as if to ward off an attack. "Very well, just remember that I'm your friend. If you want to spend your life on those acres while the lovely young damsels—like Laura Endicott—of our generation grow old, be my guest. She'll be disappointed in you. Probably not counting on marrying a farmer."

"I hardly know the lady. The wedding is set for the end of June. I shall post down to Cornwall shortly, if that makes you feel any better." Richard couldn't help but grin at the hideous grimace contorting Jerry's face.

"I'm not an ogre, Jerry. Laura will have the best I can offer."

"But not love. You're a cold fish. She'll have indigestion looking at your stern face over the coffee cup every morning."

Sir Richard made a movement as if to punch his friend, but Jerry ducked, laughing. "What you need is an adventure. Well, I hope you'll enjoy my masquerade tonight."

"I look forward to it as if it's the only event of the year worth living for," Sir Richard said sarcastically.

"What costume are you planning to wear?" Jerry asked.

"Nothing more spectacular than a pirate's outfit. I'll probably be one of ten—or more—pirates at the ball."

"Your roguish grin and hard muscles make for a good pirate," Jerry said with a chuckle. "Don't forget the eye-patch and the gold earring."

"I take it you're going as Henry the Eighth?"

"No, I'll be the court jester, and Maude, Queen Bess."

"Hmmm, jester suits you fine, my friend. You always have a ready joke on your tongue."

They stared in companionable silence across the vast park where the setting sun sent shafts of golden light among the trees. It was so peaceful that one could hear the birds chirping among the leaves, and the insects humming from plant to plant.

Suddenly, there came a shriek at the edge of the maze at the south corner of the garden. A plump middle-aged female scuttled along the path, her arms flailing. After her came a tall, slender lady, shouting, "It was only a rabbit, not a wolf, Aunt Iddy."

Sir Richard laughed at the spectacle as the older woman halted and almost toppled backward as she stepped into a dip in the path. "Who are they?" he asked Jerry.

"Lady Honoria Iddings and her charge, Miss Jillian Ashcroft of Devonshire. They are friends of my wife and staying here at the house. A pot of money there. Miss Ashcroft is worth fifty thousand pounds."

Sir Richard rubbed his chin in thought as the ladies came closer. "Ashcroft? Where have I heard that name before?"

"Probably in no favorable light. Lionel Ashcroft dabbled in the 'black' arts they say, but Miss Jillian is quite exemplary. It's hard to believe she comes from that lunatic family. Maude is quite taken with her; she says Jillian is both quick and well versed in all subjects. A charming lady, if a bit too high-spirited for my taste."

"You like them rotund, quiet, and soft. Like Maude."

Jerry tilted his head to the side as his gaze followed Miss Ashcroft's hurried approach to the terrace. "Hmm, yes. You must admit that Miss Ashcroft is too tall and too angular for real beauty. There is something about her eyes, though, as if she can see right *through* you. Still, she doesn't give you a feeling of any kind of evil. Some say she's a soothsayer. Must be that havey-cavey Ashcroft blood. She looks just like her father with her black hair and piercing eyes."

Sir Richard stared thoughtfully at the approaching ladies. Jerry was right in his assessment that Jillian Ashcroft was too tall and angular for real beauty, but her sparkling slanted eyes and intelligent face were most captivating. Something about her, an awareness, a crackling air of confidence and strength attracted him immensely.

"They call her a witch, you know," Jerry said in an undertone as the two ladies reached the steps right below them. "With such an epithet, she won't be able to find a gentleman to wed her. Maude swears there's nothing strange about Miss Ashcroft, and I tend to trust her judgment."

Miss Ashcroft let out a silvery laugh as the older woman said something, and it sounded sweet to his ears, Sir Richard thought. "She doesn't cackle, like witches ought to do," he said with a smile.

Jerry chortled. "You know a lot about witches, it seems."

The two ladies silenced as they realized they were being observed, and as Richard's gaze met Miss Ashcroft's dark eyes, something jolted inside his chest as if receiving a powerful shock. Holding his breath, he took in her black, wavy hair that looked as smooth as silk as it tried to escape the chignon, and the high cheekbones in a thin face that was interesting if not beautiful in the classical sense. Creamy, supple, golden-hued skin, like one of Jerry's peaches.

"Lady Honoria, Miss Ashcroft," Jerry introduced.

"Meet my good friend and neighbor, Sir Richard Blackwood, of Eversley."

"Eversley?" asked Lady Honoria, and stared near-sightedly at Richard. "I've heard it's one of the loveliest estates in the South Counties, and very old."

"Just the man I wanted to meet," said Miss Ashcroft without preamble and grinned.

Slightly taken aback, Sir Richard stared at her speculatively. "I had no idea you knew of my existence," he murmured, and wondered how her silky hair would feel wound around his hands. He would like to let it down and see it ripple over her shoulders. That realization startled him like nothing else, since he wasn't in the habit of viewing the intimate details of ladies' attributes. Usually the fal-lals of fashion bored him, and the females' endless chatter about the newest styles from France put him to sleep. He knew; he lived with an empty-headed old aunt, and two young female cousins, to whom he acted as guardian.

"I've known about you since the day I figured out a way to break the Ashcroft curse," she explained, not in slightest concerned about his reaction to her startling confession.

Jerry gave a belly laugh. "Listen to that, Richard. You've been targeted for mischief, for a magic spell, mayhap."

"That was unfair of you, Jerry," said the spirited Miss Ashcroft. "I don't have any magical powers."

Sir Richard doubted that as he met her scintillating gaze. "I suspect a spell would be wasted on me," he drawled. "My family is not susceptible to any supernatural turns. The Blackwoods always were a phlegmatic group."

Miss Ashcroft smiled in supreme confidence. "You

hardly seem to be phlegmatic, but then every family has its black sheep."

Jerry jostled him in the ribs. "Hear that, Richard? A black sheep."

He turned to Miss Ashcroft. "You've angered my friend. He is a paragon of virtue, never did a black-sheepish thing in his entire life—except at Oxford, perhaps."

"His life isn't over yet, is it? You never know what the future will hold," Miss Ashcroft said with a twinkle. She clapped her hand to her mouth theatrically. "How very presumptuous of me."

Sir Richard's burgeoning anger died in the glow of her mischievous grin."

"I didn't mean to insult you, Sir Richard."

He smiled ruefully. "I doubt your speech was as guileless as you pretend, but I won't hold a grudge—this once."

"Come along, Jill." Evidently flustered, Lady Honoria pulled Jillian toward the door. "We must get ready for the masked ball."

Sir Richard bowed stiffly, and he could have sworn that Miss Ashcroft gave him a wink.

Jerry chuckled and jabbed him in the side. "Richard, old fellow, I believe you're in for trouble. Delicious trouble."

Two

The lively music of stringed instruments tried to drown the chatter of the guests to no avail. The gypsy princess danced toward Sir Richard in the crush of kings, jesters, queens, and knights, her hips undulating most provocatively. He held his breath as her movements stirred a longing deep in his chest, a feeling that had never bothered him before. What was it about her that attracted him like a moth to light? Perhaps it was her dark eyes, or her gleaming hair, perhaps that bold half-smile on her lips. . . .

Glittering gold coins on chains hung around her neck and around her hair—circling the diaphanous veil of rainbow hues wound around her head. The coins tinkled as she moved and reflected the light from the many candles in the chandeliers. As she came closer, the other guests jostled her, but she only slid sinuously past, her arms making a graceful arch in the air as if dancing to an inner music.

Sir Richard clutched his wine glass hard, barely aware of the crush of people around him, everyone babbling, laughing, and flirting. He only saw the onyx gaze so firmly trained on him behind the sequined mask of the gypsy.

Her white peasant blouse revealed most of her creamy shoulders and her full ruffled silk skirt shimmered with as many hues as the veil around her head.

A slim ankle flashed as she swirled, and then she came to a stop right in front of him.

He had recognized her, of course. No other lady present had such a magnificent black mane, or so provocative a smile. She was taller than the others as well.

"Miss Ashcroft, I presume."

Jillian unfurled her vellum fan and began fanning herself. "I knew you would recognize me." She didn't sound extremely put out by the idea. "I told you this afternoon that I've been looking for you."

"But how did you identify me? There are as many as ten pirates here tonight." He paused, highly aware of her flowery scent and keen gaze. "And why not dance with one of them? I take it you've joined me in search of a dancing partner."

"No, but we would be a good match since you're the tallest pirate here." Her gaze scanned his form. "And have the broadest shoulders in this room," she added shamelessly. Taken aback, he listened to her daring speech. Surely a gently bred lady wouldn't—. "May I have the next—"

"I don't see any reason for us to dance in this dreadful squeeze, not if we want to keep our toes intact," she interrupted. She boldly tucked her arm under his. "No, I have a much better idea. Could we take a stroll somewhere, in the gallery, or on the terrace? I would like to get better acquainted."

"I'm flattered," he drawled. "I will expire with suspense if you don't tell me why you're interested in my humble person. And what about your lily-white reputation if you disappear outside on my arm? Surely it is not seemly. What will your chaperone say?"

"She can't see. . . . Anyway, we aren't exactly *disappearing.*" She flashed him an assessing look. "We're only taking a stroll among the guests. Do I have something to fear from you?"

He glanced at her in disbelief. He was nothing if not a gentleman where ladies' virtues were concerned! But instead of pointing out that fact to her, he said, "One never knows. It is a dangerous night."

She laughed and pulled him out onto the terrace. "I liked that, but don't tease me so."

They walked among other couples, he reluctantly, on edge, she lithe and carefree, not a whit shy. Red lanterns swung in the gentle breeze, scattering mists of pink light on every surface. Beside her youthful figure, he felt old and censorious even if he wasn't. It was a novel experience, one he didn't especially like. Her presence seemed to bring out only his worst traits.

Slanting a glance at her, highly aware of her creamy shoulders and graceful neck, he wondered what was going through her mind. He wasn't sure he wanted to know.

Jillian thought he looked splendid, shoulders so very broad under the dark coat, stomach flat under a tight striped jersey. So splendid in fact that a chill traveled up her spine and made her heart pound hard against her ribs. He wore a black, bushy wig and an eye patch, a red kerchief bound around his neck.

She liked his strong hands, they were decisive somehow, brooking no nonsense as he steered her around an orange tree in a tub. His jaw jutted pugnaciously and she knew she had to tread cautiously so as not to provoke his temper. She hadn't known what to expect of Sir Richard, her savior to be—but certainly not this serious, very masculine man.

He smelled clean, like fresh air and soap, and she found she didn't like gentlemen to smell of anything else.

Eyes as dark as hers he had, a surprise that gave her a feeling of kinship with him. With eyes—or one eye tonight—like a dark liquid pool, he might not be so set against her wild—if very logical—plan.

"I was charmed to discover that you knew of my existence before I knew of yours," he said politely, as the silence had grown taut between them. "I'm curious as to why."

"A very long story, Sir Richard, but perhaps I ought to tell it from the beginning." She pulled him to a wrought-iron bench beside a trailing rose bush whose pale green leaves nodded in the breeze.

He sat down beside her, crossing his black gleaming boots at the ankles, and stretching out his arm behind her on the back of the bench. "I would much rather sit here listening to you than be part of the crush inside," he said, grin flashing.

"You have a smooth way with words," Jill said with a laugh, "and I like that." She had difficulty pulling her gaze from his powerful thighs—so close to her own and encased in tight kneebreeches.

"So handsome. You're nothing like I envisioned," she added, realizing too late that she'd spoken her thoughts aloud.

"Envisioned?" His voice took on a sarcastic note. "Pray enlighten me. Have I been under your scrutiny for very long?"

A fleeting sensation of losing her confidence came over her as she looked into his implacable eye, but she took a deep breath and plunged into her tale. "No . . . yes, I'm aware of a few facts. I know you're betrothed to Miss Laura Endicott, and—"

He stiffened. "How are you acquainted with her?"

"I—my family has always known the Endicott clan. I know the Endicott Keep is located on the north side of Bodmin Moor even though I've never been there. We've been warring with the Endicotts for the last century and a half. I don't know Miss Laura, never met her, but I know she holds the solution to my vexing problem." She was silent for a moment, planning her next words carefully. "I am confronted with a very big dilemma."

"Laura has not mentioned a feud with the Ashcrofts," he said cautiously.

"Why would she dredge up ancient feuds? The old tales don't enhance the Endicott name; in fact they cast a pall over it. I have well—rather *know* that she is—a witch, one of a long line of evil sorceresses."

He bolted upright and stood over her, in a menacing manner, she thought.

"Good God, are you gone completely out of your mind!" He clamped his hands on her shoulders as if about to shake her.

"Not at all," Jill said airily, wondering how to salvage the situation. "Don't get into high dudgeon, Sir Richard. Please sit down and hear me out."

With a snort of exasperation, he flung himself onto the bench. "I suppose I have to, since Laura Endicott's fate will soon be tied to mine. Witch, indeed! You have an overly vivid imagination, Miss Ashcroft."

"As I said, it all started with our forefathers. I have an ancestor who evidently pirated the Endicott flagship in 1670. The cargo contained gold bullion and gemstones of great value. Apparently, that's how the Ashcroft fortune was founded.

"Our funds fluctuated over the centuries, but my forebears had shrewd heads on their shoulders, and kept increasing our riches—until rather recently. That notwithstanding the fact that the wife of the Endicott captain, whose ship was plundered, was a witch.

According to the old diaries and legends—and believe me, I've studied them all—she had stunning powers. She decided to avenge the Endicotts in a fearsome manner."

"Of all the bird-witted—" Sir Richard began, the sentence ending on a hissed expletive.

"It's all but true. Ask your fiancée, Miss Laura. She must know about the old legends and the hideous Endicott curse."

When he only glowered at her in the semidarkness, Jill inhaled deeply and continued. "It's said that Laura's great-grandmother could convert common metals into gold, and she conversed with the demons, even the Devil himself." Jill crossed two fingers against the evil eye. "She was capable of conjuring any spell under the sun, and the villagers trembled in fear as they listened to the thunder of explosions and watched black, blue, and yellow smoke belching from the castle on the cliff." She exhaled explosively. "It's all true."

"The Endicott Keep?" Sir Richard suddenly doubled over with a belly laugh. "You're doing it too brown, Miss Ashcroft. Do you expect me to sit here like a flat and indefinitely absorb your wild nursery tales of thunder and smoke?"

"Every word is true," she reiterated hotly. "It happened more than a hundred years ago, but the curse that the witch put on the Ashcrofts still exists. Handed down from generation to generation. Through a stone."

Sir Richard looked at her with great derision. He drawled, "Before I expire with suspense, you must explain the exact nature of this curse, and Laura's involvement."

Jill felt an urge to punch his jaw to remove the

monstrous smile from his face. She unclenched her tight fists to stop the unladylike impulse. "For all time, every family unit of the Ashcrofts will have at least two violent deaths. There have been two gruesome deaths every generation. The Ashcrofts would fail as farmers—and we have. Crops won't grow around Lindenwood, nothing except weeds, and a few trees."

"You expect me to believe this?"

"I can't convince you of anything," she said in a restrained voice. "The witch didn't count on the Ashcroft business acumen, so we prospered despite the curse. What I need at this point is your help."

"This is precious," he said scathingly. "You expect me to—? Never!"

"I knew you would be impossible! Rigid and condescending, two of the most despicable character traits in mankind." She slapped the armrest of the bench. "I detest such weakness."

"How do you expect me to behave?" he drawled maddeningly, and leaned forward to get a closer look at her face. "Hang on your every word? Admire your imagination? Not that I understand how *I* am involved in this preposterous story, nor why Laura is."

"You could always be quiet and hear me out," she said pointedly, barely able to control her temper.

He came so close that his scent overwhelmed her, confusing her thoughts momentarily. "Has someone asked you to play a prank on me tonight, Miss Ashcroft? A bet perhaps? Or is it that scoundrel Jerry who wants to pull me out of the doldrums?"

"Don't be foolish! As I said, you can help me in this." She took a deep breath to continue even though he sat so disconcertingly close to her, penetrating her gypsy disguise with the heat of his body. If she moved one inch forward, she could almost touch his lips with hers. Lips? . . . Goodness gracious!

"As . . . I . . . said before—" She shook off his intoxicating spell on her senses with difficulty.

His gaze pierced her in a most uncomfortable manner.

"Miss Laura is at the center of this problem. Over the centuries, the Endicott ladies have inherited a small stone, a stone that came from that first witch, Lucinda the Evil. I've seen drawings of it—looks like a piece of granite. Not much in the way of a family heirloom, in other words. It's set in gold filigree, and the ladies have always worn it around their necks. Brings luck to the Endicotts and holds the curse in place, and brings ruin to the Ashcrofts."

"Are you implying that Laura at present is in possession of said stone?"

"Just so! I'm delighted that your feeble mind is finally beginning to grasp the problem."

He laughed uproariously, and slammed his fist against his knee. "I've never been more entertained! If Jerry hired you to do this—You must tell him you've succeeded beyond measure. I've been diverted and bamboozled."

"Compose yourself." She stood, clenching her fists until they ached. "I cannot stand poor listeners!" As she moved as if to leave, he halted her, warm fingers closing around her arm. Heat coursed up her elbow and raced through her whole body.

"Please, you cannot leave me in suspense like this. What happens next, Miss Ashcroft?"

"*Nothing,*" she spat. "You are not fit to aid my cause. I regret that I took you into my confidence. I should have known better. You're wholly without imagination.

A gentleman of scant understanding. A bore. I've had enough of you."

She tried to pull away, but he held her tightly. Looming over her, he stared deeply into her eyes, and her legs slowly lost substance. She hadn't expected this development. For a moment she thought he would kiss her, but he backed away, still holding her arms. The chatter of nearby guests made him drop his hands to his sides in a hurry.

"Now sit down and continue. I must know what you expect of me, Miss Ashcroft." His voice had a tender inflection, and Jill softened. Perhaps he wasn't a complete bore, after all. She sat down on the edge of the bench, folding her hands tightly together.

"A servant from the Keep told one of my servants— after receiving a large bribe—that Miss Laura, like her forebears, always wears the stone around her neck on its chain. Doesn't take it off at night, or when she changes her dresses. As long as it hangs there it has the power to ruin the lives of the Ashcrofts. I might be the next victim, or my odious cousin, Alvin.

"Father was the last to die in a violent accident. Alvin's father drowned when his ship went under, ruining that branch of the Ashcrofts. More cargo ships have sunk for the Ashcrofts than for any other shipping families in Devon and Cornwall."

He rubbed his jaw and peered at her, not unkindly. "It's evident you believe this story. But what do you want me to do?"

"You must get Miss Laura to give you the stone. You will then give it to me, and I shall follow the instruction on how to break the curse. Father came across a solution in his studies of witchcraft, but he died before he had a chance to try it."

In her eagerness, she placed her hand on Sir

Richard's thigh, and he didn't move away. "However, we don't have much time. At the next full moon, the ceremony must be done. We've only three weeks to fulfill my father's calculations. Then, *then*," she emphasized, "the Ashcrofts will be free. You will help me, won't you, Sir Richard? You're my only hope."

He clasped her hand in his warm grip, evidently thinking hard. A fiery sensation robbed her of her breath as he brushed her knuckles with his lips. She'd never before been so overwhelmed by the proximity of a gentleman. She wasn't sure this feeling was beneficial to her plan, but it didn't matter. What mattered was that she'd told him about her plight. "I'll show you the old diaries, and Father's calculations based on an old letter that one of the Endicott witches sent to my great-great-grandfather. She must have had one glimmer of light in her dark soul as she hinted at the possible annulment of the curse. My ancestor died, however, before he had a chance to dissolve the curse."

Ominously silent, he stared hard at her, and she continued.

"Since you're betrothed to Miss Laura, you must convince her to part with the stone and give it to me. I don't care how you do it." She waited tensely for his reaction.

"Are you truly implying that Laura Endicott is a . . . witch?" He gave an incredulous laugh.

"She is. Why, she's always closeted at that sinister Keep. As far as I know, she has never been to London, or had a season. Nobody ever goes there."

"Have you visited the Endicott Keep?"

Jill shook her head. "An Ashcroft won't cross through the gatehouse. It could be very dangerous."

"Ahh, you wouldn't be that craven, Miss Ashcroft. You must go and slay the dragon yourself."

"I hoped you would do that for me," she said breathlessly.

A smile still lurked at the corners of his handsome—if slightly derisive—mouth, and Jill could tell that he was struggling to keep from laughing out loud.

He spoke. "As far as I know, Laura Endicott is a well-behaved, reputable young woman. She always behaves decorously in my presence. I've heard nothing to the effect that she dabbles in black magic. You, however, have not such an angelic reputation, Miss Ashcroft. In fact, I've heard from more than one source that you are probably the witch in question, not Laura. Why should I help you? Perhaps you mean to destroy her, not the other way around."

"Very well . . . I can't convince you to believe me, but I know how you might be persuaded to help me. After all, isn't your estate struggling since you took it over from your father? Could you use a few thousand pounds to right the wrongs at Eversley? I'd be willing to pay for your services."

He stiffened and dropped her hand abruptly. "Money? Are you gone completely mad, Miss Ashcroft?"

"I'm not jesting. I'm prepared to—"

"Miss Ashcroft! It's unthinkable. I won't accept funds from you."

He rose. "Why don't you solicit the help of your cousin, Alvin Ashcroft? I believe he would be the gentleman to ask—since his very life might be threatened by the curse."

"My lily-livered cousin has only one thought in his mind—how to get his hands on my inheritance. He has nothing but Lindenwood to his name, and as you well know, an estate consumes considerable funds for its upkeep." She took a deep breath. "Besides, Alvin detests me. Like you, he believes I might have magical powers, and he's afraid of what I'll do. It's because I can sense a lie before it comes, and he lies constantly."

"You don't live an easy life, it seems," Sir Richard said with renewed sarcasm.

"I don't brood endlessly over my problems; I try to solve them. Is there something wrong with that?"

He shook his head. "It's only that you don't seem to have problems like us—regular—people."

"And that makes me a witch?" Her anger surged to the surface. "That was ungentlemanly of you! I'm not a witch."

"Neither is Miss Laura. You're sadly deluded if you believe that."

"I'm not surprised that you take her side in this matter, and I don't hold it against you, but you must help me."

"I certainly have no inclination to do so. Not now, not ever." He gave her a mocking bow. "I thank you for an entertaining half hour. I shall tell Miss Laura what you've told me, and if she so desires, she can hand you the stone—or you can buy it from her. If it exists."

"She won't part with it! I see that I must resort to more dire measures. If you don't help me—"

"How do you know if you don't try to see her? She might give you the blasted stone, and the matter can be settled."

"Her oldest heirloom? I told you, Miss Laura wouldn't part with that stone for anything, except perhaps give it to you. When you're wed, you control her estate. Perhaps you can convince her—"

"Miss Ashcroft!" He shook his head. "I'm beginning to tire of your pigheadedness. You won't be able to elicit my aid with bribes, nor by bullying. You don't have a chance of turning me against my fiancée. Besides, I can't very well rip the cursed stone from her neck if she doesn't wish it."

Jill heaved a deep, exasperated sigh. "I don't want to resort to underhanded tactics, but it looks like I might have to now. I suspect I will have to play out another card to secure your cooperation."

He crossed his arms over his chest. "And what might that be? Don't say you are threatening me!"

"Be that as it may, I know of the scandal that you've desperately tried to conceal since your sister died." She lowered her voice to a near whisper. "I found out about it since I was in Belgium at the time of your sister's confinement and subsequent death. I discovered from the dear soul herself that she was *enceinte,* but not married."

Three

Jill felt soiled as she threatened him with that sordid scandal. Never in her life would she betray the woman—Miss Letitia Blackwood—who'd become her friend that summer in Belgium a year ago. But now her own life was perhaps in danger, and she had to secure his help any way she could to save future Ashcrofts.

Sir Richard was glowering at her, and a frisson of fear shot up her spine. She suspected that he had a violent temper, and she sensed that it would be very uncomfortable to be at the receiving end of it.

"I have no desire to dredge that up needlessly. Letitia was an unfortunate young lady, and I understand your eagerness to keep her pregnancy a secret. I was so sorry that she didn't survive the ordeal of giving birth."

He gripped her shoulders and shook her until she grew dizzy. "You have no right to mention my sister's name, Miss Ashcroft," he growled under his breath. "At this moment I have a powerful urge to strangle you and forever silence your careless tongue. You're nothing but a conniving madwoman, and I'm tired of your company. If you ever threaten me again, I shall make your life such a hell that it will make the Ashcroft curse pale in comparison."

"So you do believe my story?" she said in elation.

"I do not, damn you!" In a rush of exhaled anger, he dropped his hands, and strode toward the doors. "Leave me alone from now on!"

"Wait!" she called after him. "We haven't finished; we must discuss this further." She hurried after him.

"I won't exchange another word with you, Miss Witch! If you as much as look at me again this evening, I shall make good my threat."

Jill halted, watching helplessly as he slammed through the doorway, almost toppling a flower urn on a pedestal. Her threat had gone unheeded. She admitted it had been a low blow, but she was desperate, and he hadn't understood that.

Didn't he care about the future of the Ashcrofts? Then again, why should he? But didn't he mind the fact that Laura descended from a long line of witches? Evidently not. He seemed to be a cold-hearted bore, if a very masculine, attractive one. He might as well marry an evil witch and be cursed forever!

"By all that is good, what shall I try next?"

She sank down on the top marble step leading down to the weakly illuminated garden. The scent of honeysuckle lingered in the mild spring night. A night for lovers, and she was sitting alone. The gentlemen were probably frightened to go outside with her in the dark . . . afraid that she might turn them into horned toads.

She held back a giggle. Bah! She'd never felt more powerless in her life. Lily-livered lot, the Celtborn guests. What now? She couldn't give up without at least trying once more to win Sir Richard's help. She was certain he could persuade Laura Endicott to part with her magic stone.

* * *

The following morning Sir Richard was still fuming as he thought about the confrontation with Miss Ashcroft. As soon as he'd been able to leave the Celtborns' party without appearing rude, he had left. It was a relief to be back at Eversley. Thank God, he hadn't laid eyes on that treacherous miss again! She had no manners, didn't know in the least how to behave properly in polite gatherings. Her upbringing was sadly lacking.

At first he'd been intrigued by her grand imagination that had contrived such an involved story for his entertainment. When he'd realized that she truly believed in the rubbish, he'd been appalled. Who in his right mind would consider ancient curses and old wives' tales important? Clearly Miss Ashcroft was touched in her upper works.

After spending a sleepless night reliving the old pain that the memory of Letitia brought forth, he sat at his desk as the morning sun shone brightly over the papers spread out before him. He was dressed in a shabby corduroy riding jacket, buckskins, and top boots since he planned to ride over the hill to one of the cottages and examine a herd of sheep.

He'd been unable to eat his breakfast, his mind revolving around the scandal that he thought buried and forgotten. But it never would be. . . . The old wounds would open again and again to remind him of his loss, his excruciating guilt as he'd let his sister die far away from home with only her aunt in attendance. Aside from Miss Ashcroft, perhaps others had witnessed Letitia's humiliation. Who would come next and demand a favor for his silence?

Unease filled him until he felt slightly queasy. The scandal was one year old, and so far he'd been able to keep it a secret. If only he'd been firm enough, circumspect enough, to stop his wild younger sister's romantic trysts with the opposite sex. He'd been too involved in the estate, too worried about the future to fully understand her recklessness. His aunt, Letitia's chaperone, had turned a blind eye to the goings-on.

At the time of Letitia's disastrous affair with an army captain—the father of her stillborn child—Sir Richard had been grieving the death of their parents. She'd shown her grief by becoming more unmanageable, and throwing herself into one flirtation after the other. He hadn't been there to temper her grief. That guilt would eat him until the day he died.

Aunt Cordelia had been no match for Letitia, who ignored all strictures. He'd been forced to send his sister abroad to await the birth of the child who would be instantly turned over to adoptive parents. It had never come to that, of course. Letitia had lost her life, and so had the child.

Sorrow twisted in his gut, and he held his breath for a long moment. What folly! If only he'd kept her at home! Gossip be damned! Mayhap she would have survived.

If this scandal were to become public knowledge, he would be unable to find suitable husbands for his young wards, Miss Lenore and Miss Primrose Hadleigh, cousins from his mother's side of the family. In his current predicament of straitened circumstances, they needed to make good matches next season when he planned to bring them to London. Now the sharp tongue of that sly madcap from Devon threatened their precarious future.

"Damn you, Miss Ashcroft!" he said and punched his desk so hard that the ink horn jumped and the goose quill fell over, spattering ink spots all over his papers. In a foul mood, he stalked to the open French doors and stepped into the quiet park of Eversley. He inhaled deeply, loving the clean earthy scent of his domain. Eversley was all he'd ever cared for, and he had to find a way to return it to its former prosperity before they all went under and had to sell the estate.

Sir Richard wasn't the only one who'd spent a sleepless night. Drinking strong coffee, Jillian battled a headache alone at the Celtborns' breakfast table. Most of the guests were still sleeping off the excesses of champagne. Most would not emerge before the day was old, and then start the festivities all over. Aunt Iddy would not rise until ten o'clock, and it was only eight in the morning.

Somehow, a dark veil seemed to hang over everything, as if the sun didn't have the power to warm the earth. She knew it was nothing but her imagination playing tricks, but the threat hovered nevertheless. Sometimes she could sense trouble before it happened, and this was one of those moments.

Pushing back her chair, she rose abruptly. She couldn't remain inactive, letting the day slip by without some effort to solve her problems.

She met Lady Celtborn in the doorway. "Ah, you're up early, Jillian. Didn't you enjoy a late night at the ball? It was such a success!"

Lacking her usual vigor, Jillian greeted her rotund hostess. "I enjoyed it immensely." She indicated the sunny morning outside. "I thought I would take advantage of this lovely weather to get some exercise. May I ride one of your horses?"

Lady Celtborn patted her arm. "Of course! No need to ask. The head groom will select a suitable mount, and he'll send someone to accompany you. If you ride through the spinney, you'll get to the sea. You'll pass Eversley, and voilà, the coast!"

Jillian hurried upstairs and waited patiently while Jane, her maid, brushed her riding habit. Due to the glorious English victory at Waterloo, the cut of her coat was inspired by the dashing Hussars' uniform, tight scarlet cloth with gold epaulets and gold braid closings across her chest. She wore a white skirt, and her small round black hat had a veil and two curling ostrich feathers. Her riding boots gleamed as brilliantly as those of any general. She knew red set off her black hair to perfection. Surely there was nothing wrong in looking her best, was there?

Dressed for her outing, she hurried down the stairs carrying a riding crop and an old leather-bound book. Eversley was on the way to the coast. She could see no reason why she shouldn't stop there and have another chat with the stubborn Sir Richard Blackwood, even if he was eating his way through a hearty country breakfast.

A traveling chaise pulled up to the door as she was heading toward the stables. To her chagrin, she recognized her cousin Alvin's bloodless countenance in the window. His lank blond hair looked mussed as if he'd been traveling for some time. If that lazy young wastrel had bestirred himself to leave London in his creaking old chaise, he must be in a pickle of some sort.

Jillian didn't doubt for a moment that he was in search of her—or rather her money, which often enough had placated some irate merchant on her cousin's behalf.

Before he could catch a glimpse of her, she hurried around to the back and the stables. She would confront Alvin later, a meeting she didn't exactly look forward to. She didn't look with great anticipation toward her confrontation with Sir Richard either, but she could not shirk her duty to the Ashcrofts.

She clutched her father's dog-eared journal containing the old letter under her arm. Perhaps it would persuade Sir Richard if her pleas failed once again.

Eversley stretched before her as she rode out of the woods. Set at the edge of the gentle downs, it was a rambling brick structure with a steep slate roof and many mullioned windows. All walls were partially covered with ivy, and the park consisted of orderly boxwood hedges, flower borders, and rock gardens. A fountain tinkled in the somnolent air, and birds took their morning bath in the shallow marble basin. They dashed into the water and ruffled their feathers in a most abandoned manner, Jill thought, and remarked as much to the groom accompanying her at a respectable distance.

"Do you know if Sir Richard is at home?" she asked as they rode together onto a knoll that gave them a view of the glittering Channel half a mile away.

"I wouldn't know, Miss."

"We'll ride up to the door and enquire. If he isn't at home, we might as well go all the way to the coast."

Sir Richard was at home, and after sending her groom and the horses to the stables, she handed the butler her card. He left her to cool her heels in the silent hallway. The house was old, the wall paneling carved and inlaid with exotic woods. She saw a glimpse of a salon furnished with an enormous Oriental carpet and damask-upholstered sofas and chairs. Another door led to a library, a door through which the butler had entered and then closed behind him. Sir Richard waited inside; she could sense him. Her shoulders stiffened as she anticipated the fight ahead—that is if he agreed to see her. He might not, and then what?

Clasping the journal under her arm, she tried to find the consolation in the work her father had executed with so much love and dedication. Sir Richard must be made to understand the importance of her quest. . . .

Concentrating on a tall, stained glass window at the other end of the hall, she steeled herself for the battle to win him over. The sunshine slanted through the panes, making multi-colored squares on the floor. The old house was lovely, she thought, steeped in peace and dignity. She felt quite drawn to the peace here.

When the butler cut into her reverie, she jumped with fright. Her heartbeat fluttered erratically.

"This way, Miss Ashcroft. Sir Richard has five minutes to spare."

"Only five?"

Jillian took a deep breath and plunged into the "lion's lair." The air hung heavy with suspicion even if she couldn't see Sir Richard right away. She felt him as keenly as if he'd been touching her. In this room he was king, and she the beggar.

He was standing with his back toward her staring out a window. The library was well stocked and a loving craftsman had carved molding around the ceiling in the style of the previous century.

Aside from two French doors, the leaded windows had diamond-shaped panes of old glass that contorted the view. The room had a low, beamed ceiling, and comfortable furniture—a masculine room filled with a clutter of brass and leather. Hunting prints hung above the fireplace.

"If you've come to threaten me, you might as well

turn around and leave this minute," he said as the butler had left them alone and closed the door.

"I didn't come to cause a commotion; I came to reason with you, and if that's impossible, a threat—"

She became silent as he turned around, facing her. He looked haggard under his sun-bronzed complexion, and his eyes stared at her as if from the depth of a deep, dark pit. He hadn't slept well, she concluded, and she understood why. An unfamiliar feeling made her choke up, and her heart hammered like a wild thing in her chest. She held out the journal.

"I brought this for you to see, and you have to read the letter inside. It will take away any doubt on your part."

He laughed dryly. "You're still maintaining that the Ashcrofts are cursed?"

"That is correct. Perhaps I can finally make you believe me in the bright light of day. I'm not hoaxing you."

He stared at her incredulously. "And if I don't believe you—?"

"Then you're more unimaginative than I ever envisioned. A deadly dull bore."

"Insults won't help your mission, but hardly anyone would want to admit being a deadly dull bore." His voice heavily laced with sarcasm, he indicated the well-worn leather chair in front of his desk.

"Please sit, Miss Ashcroft." He glanced briefly toward the door. "I'm not surprised to find you unchaperoned."

Jill dared to smile. "Does that make you uneasy? You're very much bound to convention, Sir Richard."

"And you not at all. Which is a pity." His words heavy with accusation taunted her, but she didn't say anything to defend herself.

She held the journal toward him. "Please take a few minutes to study this. At the end there's a summary of my father's findings. I shall await your company in the garden." Without another word, she left the house through the French doors and strolled along a sandy path. Her heartbeat would not calm down, and her face felt uncommonly hot.

On the outside, she was calm, but when she lifted her hand, she noticed that it trembled.

As she came upon a bench in a rose arbor, she encountered a tiny middle-aged lady who wore a thick wool gown despite the warm summer temperature. Her small body was of slender proportions, but her hands looked large and unexpectedly capable. Her face held an expression of sweet vacuity touched with grief.

"Dear me!" she said, clasping her hand to her heart. "You took me by surprise, young lady."

"I'm sorry if I frightened you. I'm Jillian Ashcroft. I'm here to discuss business with Sir Richard."

The older lady's eyes grew round. Wisps of gray hair fell from the untidy bun under her cap, and her hands stilled on her knitting, something brown and bulky, a scarf perhaps.

"Oh, my . . . business?" the older lady said vaguely. "I'm Cordelia Hampton, Sir Richard's aunt. You're the one who threatened to tell the world. . . . Aren't you?" Her voice trailed off.

"Sir Richard told you about me?"

"Richard has no secrets from me. I've known him since he was born. He's as dear to me as if he were my own son." Miss Hampton scrutinized Jill with quick eyes. "You don't look vicious, but then appearances can be deceiving."

Jill felt Miss Hampton's suspicion wash over her. "I

assure you, I don't make a habit of threatening people for personal gain. I assure you, I'm not vicious."

"Let me tell you, young miss, Richard is a fine man. He's always struggling to better our lot here at Eversley. I don't hold with underhanded tricks, Miss Ashcroft. Remember that! And I don't hold with dredging up past sorrows. Richard has suffered enough."

"Once again, I assure you—" Jill began, coloring.

"Richard has two young wards. If any hint of scandal reaches the *ton* they'll be forever shunned from the portals of polite society."

Jill cringed, heavy with guilt. "Surely it isn't as bad as that. They are not guilty of any crime. And I wouldn't do—"

"Say no more. It's clear that you don't understand the importance of a pure reputation, but I do, and Richard does."

Jill realized it was pointless to argue with Miss Hampton. Somehow this conversation made her see Sir Richard in a different light. He was caring rather than cynical, dedicated rather than bull-headed. And he hurt inside. But he was still Sir Richard, stingy with his favors.

"I . . . I believe he'll make a success of anything he decides to pursue," Jill said diplomatically, thinking about the prospect of gaining the magic stone.

The tiny woman rose, staring down at Jill, who stood a head taller. "See that you don't destroy his future, or that of those who depend on him."

Jill swallowed hard and misery filled her chest. Steps crunched on the gravel behind her. "Of course not! I wouldn't dream—"

"Aunt Cordelia? Are you badgering Miss Ashcroft?"

asked Sir Richard, frowning as he joined them, the journal in one hand.

Miss Hampton snorted. "Only pointing out a few truths to her. I won't have her threatening you."

Jillian clamped the door to her conscience shut and squared her shoulders. "Sir Richard baldly refuses to discuss any acceptable strategies with me. I have no choice but to use every weapon in my arsenal."

"Well, I never!" Miss Hampton elbowed her aside and moved away in high dudgeon.

"Anything to gain your goal, Miss Ashcroft?"

Jill's anger flared. "I offered to pay you, Sir Richard, fair and square for services rendered, and you refused." She tore the journal from his grip. "Did you read the summary?"

Sir Richard's eyes glittered like frost. "I did. Your father must have been a great philosopher, but nothing more than that. I've found nothing to convince me to take up with your cause. I grant you the legend is there in the old words, but it has no substance to it. Anyhow, I have no desire to involve my fiancée in something unsavory."

Jill flinched. She'd never heard anyone speak in so derogatory a fashion about her father and his work. It felt as if someone had poured a bucket of icy water over her head.

"Don't you understand anything? Father . . ." she began, her voice faltering. Hot tears gathered in her eyes, and she lowered her gaze. "You don't know what it has been like to live with the curse, never knowing what evil might happen next, who would die next."

"Woe is me," he chided, and handed her a handkerchief, which she pushed away. "Your new tricks won't break me down. I've seen enough female tears to last a lifetime."

"You're monstrous, Sir Richard," Jill said, fighting an urge to flee. She faced him, staring into those mistrusting dark eyes. "And since you are, I shall make good on my threat. If you don't help me, I shall tell the world—"

He gripped her arms and squeezed hard. She stood her ground, staring defiantly into his rising anger.

"Will you?" he asked menacingly.

She wanted to scream, Yes! Deep inside she knew, as she'd known all along, that she couldn't do such a dastardly thing as to ruin Sir Richard's life. He hadn't done anything wrong, other than making things difficult for her.

"Will you?" he repeated, now shaking her.

She exhaled slowly, facing complete failure. "No," she whispered between stiff lips, and he dropped his arms. He looked tired and drawn as all his anger seeped away.

"No, I don't think I could ever do that," she said again, stronger now.

"I had to hear it with my own ears," he said. "And since you've promised not to ruin my family's reputation, I promise to take up this matter with Miss Laura at the earliest convenient time. I'm going down to Cornwall in a few days."

Jill brightened, her hopes soaring anew. "I knew there was a way to convince you. Mark my words, she'll tell you the same story about the curse."

"How can I reach you after I've spoken to her?"

"I always spend one summer month at Lindenwood with Aunt Iddy and Cousin Alvin."

He glanced into the distance. "Perhaps I can unite you with Miss Laura at a neutral spot and discuss this matter. She has certainly never mentioned the curse to me."

"Why would she confide in you about the curse? You're literally a stranger, and her ancestry isn't something to be very proud of even if she hails from a very old family."

He gave a hollow laugh. "And yours is?"

Jillian raised her chin a notch. "I'm trying to make a new life for the Ashcrofts, to wash away the evil of centuries. Miss Laura has done nothing to change the situation, so I will. That's why I need your help so desperately. I now see a glimmer of hope." He muttered something under his breath, probably something vile.

She turned away as if to leave. "Good morning, Sir Richard. I expect to hear from you soon." She paused on the path and met his penetrating gaze.

When he didn't say anything, she added. "I pity you that you must marry Laura Endicott, a witch descended from Lucinda the Evil. It won't be an easy life." As she hurried toward the stables, she could hear his incredulous laugh on the wind.

Four

Endicott Keep had rested at the edge of Bodmin Moor, on the jagged cliffs over the restless waters of the Irish Sea, for centuries. The remnants of a moat that had mostly been filled in with dirt surrounded the old gray stone castle, whose crenellated walls and grim towers spoke of a more violent time when the landlords had to protect themselves against intruders. Parts of the castle had fallen or been torn down to accommodate more recent architecture, but its ancient history lingered in every line and every rock.

Sir Richard rode up to the Keep's front entrance, his emotions mixed as he thought of seeing his betrothed. Laura was one of the sweetest young ladies he'd ever met, but also somewhat passive, something he had difficulty reconciling as he himself had more energy than he knew what to do with. He liked her peaceful demeanor, but he doubted they had much in common.

He had promised his father to take care of her, and he never went back on his promises, but a young sheltered lady could only hold so much allure for a man of the world. She was almost a decade younger than he, and she hadn't even had the opportunity for a Season in London to gain some Town polish, but she never complained about any kind of lack.

The elderly aunt with whom she lived had not seen

the inside of London in the last forty years, he suspected. He knocked on the ancient oak door and Brumley, the butler, opened it in a moment.

"Sir Richard," he said gravely. "We received the missive about your imminent arrival. Miss Endicott is eagerly awaiting your presence—in the stables."

"Stables?"

"Yes, sir. She is overseeing the birth of a litter of puppies."

"More animals," Sir Richard said with a sigh.

"Aye, you know how she loves the four-footed of all kinds," Brumley said with a sage smile.

Sir Richard lifted his shoulders in a fatalistic shrug. "It's only lately I've found out to what extent. She writes about nothing else. I'll walk down there." Which he did as he thought of how Laura had a special knack in caring for animals. For some reason they trusted her implicitly, and he'd witnessed wounded foxes and rabbits allow her to touch them and soothe them in their pain.

She also seemed to have special abilities to heal them quickly with her ointments and tinctures. Not that he had any idea what they contained, but she always found recourse for the alleviation of suffering.

He saw her immediately as he stepped away from the shadow cast by the door. She sat in a pile of hay at one end of the stables and watched over a beautiful harrier bitch that already had four chubby puppies crawling over her stomach. Laura looked charming with her blond hair in an untidy knot of cascading curls and an old straw hat on her head. Her periwinkle blue muslin dress looked faded and well worn. Laura had no inkling about fashion, nor did she seem to care. A streak of dust ran down her cheek and her shoes had seen better days.

She wore an air of innocence that played in her blue eyes and her gentle smile. Part of him wanted to question why she'd rather sit on a pile of hay and watch over a dog when she could be playing the pianoforte or watercolor painting, but he truly couldn't find fault with her love for animals. It was as if she'd been blessed differently than other people, and the animals knew it.

And clearly, her mother had done nothing to instill any sense of propriety in Laura.

The young woman lifted her head for a moment and glanced at him as he approached. For a second she looked confused, and she placed a hand to her hat as if to feel if she appeared presentable in her old garb, but then promptly forgot about it.

"Richard! What a pleasure." Her whole face beamed, and he couldn't but feel gratified by her enthusiasm. Mayhap his more tender feelings would grow in time, but he could not return her smile with the same vigor even if it looked as if the chit truly enjoyed his presence.

"Laura," he greeted her and pecked a kiss on her hand as she held it out toward him. "I should've known I'd find you here—"

"—in the part of Endicott Keep that is most dear to my heart," she filled in. She pointed at the laboring bitch that seemed comfortable enough without assistance—in his opinion. "Jewel will have another two I believe. Six is a lot, but she's a sturdy dog, and a good mother. I know from her past litters."

"She looks like a good hunting dog," Sir Richard said and bent down to stroke the soft floppy ears. Jewel looked at him with trust and slapped her tail against the blanket on which she lay.

"I'd say one of the best—if we ever hunted, which we don't." Laura's face glowed as she glanced at the bitch. "I helped to deliver her into the world four years ago, and her mother was a great dog."

"At least she appears healthy. More often than not do I find you working with wounded animals."

She nodded. "That's right, but you haven't visited me that many times."

He felt somewhat guilty as he thought of how he'd avoided her in the past, but that had to change now that they were preparing for the wedding. "Your correspondence has been very entertaining and informative."

She beamed.

Their nuptials loomed in June, and he had only one month to really get to know his bride. He'd been dragging his feet as someone walking toward his execution. Perhaps it was something all gentlemen felt when facing parson's mousetrap.

She pushed her hand through his arm, and together they walked out into the sunshine. Bits of straw clung to her gown, and he gingerly pulled them off as she shook the dust out of her skirts.

"I must look a fright," she commented, blushing.

He noted the few brown freckles sprinkled over the bridge of her nose, and his gaze fell farther down, to the hollow of her throat where an inconspicuous necklace hung.

Miss Ashcroft's vivid tale of the curse came back to him.

He drew a sharp breath as he watched the crude gray stone set in stingy gold filigree. It was as if the jeweler had had second thoughts or been in haste when he anchored the stone to the metal. At certain angles of the light he could make out symbols carved into the gray surface, but not what they depicted. The chain looked very old and worn.

"Laura, I have never seen you wear that piece of jewelry," he said, wondering if she knew it was the "magic" Endicott pendant. She must know.

"I always wear it, Richard, but sometimes I tuck it inside my dress if it doesn't match rest of my attire, which it rarely does. 'Tis not of a popular style, nor is it a gem that has any value."

Sir Richard felt a chill travel up his spine. "It's a curious piece." He hoped she would elaborate, and reached out to touch it but had second thoughts. He dropped his hand to his side. "It looks very old."

"I've had it all my life. It's a family heirloom—an odd one."

"Not exactly diamonds and sapphires," he concluded, "but an heirloom is an heirloom."

"I don't know exactly how old it is. It has belonged to the Endicott women for a century or more, but I've found out very little about it. Mother was vague on the history of the piece, but I've been strangely drawn to it all my life. Must be the fact that it's so ancient."

"I hope to put something else in its place. A ruby set in gold perhaps, or a sapphire to match your eyes."

She blushed. "No need for that, Richard. Besides, I don't like rubies."

"How can it be?"

"They are ostentatious."

"A sapphire it'll be then, with diamonds. We'll create some new heirlooms."

She looked pleased, but somewhat withdrawn at the same time.

"If you would but put that old rock into my care I can have it cleaned and the chain replaced." He watched her closely for any kind of reaction.

She fingered the pendant then tucked it inside her

bodice quickly as if loath to let his gaze linger on her throat any longer. "That's not necessary."

He swallowed his disappointment. Acquiring the pendant would not be easy. "Looks like common gray stone," he said.

"It might be. If precious, it's in its crude state. I believe it's a talisman of protection, something a family member purchased abroad long ago and brought home to his wife. The Endicotts were explorers and seafarers."

"Do you know what any of the symbols mean?"

She shook her head. "No, but that isn't important to me; it's the feeling of comfort it gives me that matters to me. My family, especially Mother, didn't speak much of the past; she acted as if she was rather ignorant about a lot of things. I believe she had interest in fripperies of all kinds, but not in history. As you know, my father died when I was very young. He most likely knew more about the family's past. There must be accounts in the library, but I've mostly been studying the books about animal husbandry."

She gave him a long searching look. "I pray you won't have any objections to me pursuing my interest in animals."

"No . . . but you are a rather unusual woman."

"I am?"

"You have lived sheltered for so long, Laura. Sooner or later you'll have to take up your duties as a hostess in polite society, which means you can't spend your days in barns and stables."

She hung her head momentarily. "I understand, and I know I sorely lack in the area of dealing with the *haute monde,* but I can learn."

Sir Richard heard a snort behind him and a frantic flapping of wings and turned around. To his amazement, he found that Hector, one of the oldest horses that had been put out to pasture, a mangy dog, two kittens, and a gaggle of geese, had followed them up to the house. As Laura laughed, Hector nuzzled her hand, and she stroked the white blaze on his forehead.

"They always follow me around," she said. "But I don't know how Hector got out of the pasture. The gate must be open."

"He probably knows how to open it after all these years," Sir Richard said wryly. "And it's clear that he adores you."

She nodded. "Ever since I was born, Hector . . . well, speaks to me."

"In a horsy kind of voice?" he ventured gently.

She blushed. "I know it sounds mad . . . but I can actually feel what he's thinking."

He let the revelation sink in and realized he believed her, however unreal the statement. Laura would not lie; he believed she was incapable of lying. "You have known him for a very long time, and I'm certain animals have feelings just like us."

She patted his arm. "That's what I like about you, Richard. You never chide me. You have never shown me anything but respect, and you listen to me."

"There's no other way to be, Laura."

They looked at each other, and Richard hoped there would be some kind of discovery about their deeper feelings, but Laura only smiled her sunny smile that didn't really invite him in even if it didn't reject him.

He continued. "As long as we're honest, we can find solutions to anything."

"I'm glad we get to know each other better before the wedding," she said simply. "I could never marry someone who didn't understand my love for animals."

He was about to respond, but a commotion at the front door interrupted him. Someone had arrived, and he recognized the neighboring lord, Viscount Sandhurst, a young buck who had a reputation in London as a gamester and a Lothario.

"Julian!" Laura cried and ran forward. "I thought you'd abandoned us completely for the Metropolis."

Julian, Lord Sandhurst, laughed, one of those deep velvety laughs that would charm any woman, Richard suspected.

"I would never abandon *you*, Laura. You're practically family," Julian said as he touched her cheek with one fingertip.

She smiled adoringly and Sir Richard felt a stab of foreboding in his stomach. Competition, or what was going on? But his betrothed was still promised to him, he thought. Nothing had changed in that respect, but the situation had a sense of imbalance, and he didn't know how to interpret it.

"You're the big bullying brother I never had." Laura laughed, that beautiful infectious laugh that Richard had heard the first time he'd met her, but it still didn't take away from the sense that something was askew. He should question her but realized that he didn't know enough about Laura to put any questions to her, especially questions about other men that might suggest he harbored jealousy.

Blasted nuisance, he thought.

The suspicion about Laura's feelings for her neighbor bothered him, as he wanted to truly know the woman he was about to marry before their wedding day—not have to deal with romantic complications. He inhaled sharply, hoping to release the tension in his chest.

"I wondered if you'd gone to London for good,"

she said to the stranger, who wasn't a stranger to her, Richard had to remember. "You didn't tell me you were leaving, Julian."

"I didn't know I had to leave on such short notice," the viscount replied. "Pressing business."

Surely, Richard thought, remembering how many times he'd used that same expression when he didn't want to tell the truth. Laura's face held a look of disappointment, and that bothered him too.

"I've returned bearing gifts," Julian said and threw a speculative glance in Richard's direction. "And I see that you have company." He held out his hand. "You must be Sir Richard."

Laura introduced them and Richard returned the hard handshake.

"You're very fortunate to have won Laura's affection," Julian said, and Richard thought he detected an edge in the other man's voice.

"Yes, I am."

Uncomfortable silence fell, and Laura returned her attention to the animals that had followed her. She petted an orange cat winding its body around her legs. "Aunt Penny heard that one of your mares had taken ill," she said to no one in particular.

"Yes," Julian said. "She sprained a fetlock." He paused, looking pained. "I know you're very gifted healing their ailments," he pointed to the animals, "but so is Henry, the groom. I can't take you away from your duties here, Laura."

She made a grimace as if sorely disappointed, and Richard wondered if it'd be a huge mistake to marry her. He didn't want his wife to be yearning for some other gentleman.

"What did you bring me from London, Julian?"

He brought out a square package wrapped in

brown paper and string. Gleefully, she tore off the paper, revealing a small exquisite painting of a horse and a dog. "Thank you!" she cried. "'Tis beautiful. You know me so well."

She gave him a chaste kiss on the cheek.

"I remember when you were born, Laura," Julian said, his eyes glittering with something other than affection. "You had a pair of lungs that have not been rivaled since."

"You're exaggerating I'm sure," she replied, gazing at the painting.

"How are your nuptial plans progressing?" Julian turned to Richard. "If you need anything from my succession houses, Sir Richard, please don't hesitate."

"We would not want to impose on your goodwill, Sandhurst. I'm certain everything is under control." Finding himself beholden in any way to Viscount Sandhurst was the last thing he wanted to do. He took Laura's arm. "We shouldn't be rude to your neighbor, my dear."

She beamed at him. "You're right of course. Julian, you have to stay for dinner." She took hold of her old friend's arm with one hand and Sir Richard's with the other and led them to the entrance of the Keep.

Richard knew he had a long uncomfortable evening ahead of him, and he would not have a chance to talk further with Laura without the viscount listening in. Damned nuisance, but it couldn't be helped. This was a time when he had to put Laura's wishes before his own if he were ever to win her trust and her love.

Jillian stared at Cousin Alvin's pale face. He'd always reminded her of a fish, with his pasty skin and his milky blue eyes. Perhaps someone would call her uncharitable in her criticisms, but Alvin didn't just look like a fish, he had the cold and clammy disposition of one. Especially now as he stood staring at her motionlessly, his nose making noises every time he took a breath.

"I've told you again and again that you can't wring another groat from me, Alvin. I've helped you enough as it is, and it's about time you start looking for ways to make Lindenwood as profitable as it was in earlier days."

"I have absolutely no interest in crop rotation or cattle raising," her cousin said peevishly. "And 'tis monstrously unfair that you should have all the funds when I'm the one to carry the name to the next line."

That is if you can find someone to marry you, she thought unkindly as he eyed her from tip to toe speculatively. "You have to look for a suitable wife."

"There's nothing to stop us from getting legshackled," he pointed out for the fifty-ninth time.

"Except the simple fact—for the sixtieth time—that I won't have you," she cried, her patience hanging by a thin thread. "Why don't you stop pestering me? If you can't find a way to make Lindenwood prosperous again, find an heiress to marry. Needless to say, there are many of them on the marriage mart."

"Long in the tooth and horse faced, yes," he whined, "there are plenty, but no one whose face I would want to see upon rising in the morning."

"A man of desperate circumstances, aren't you?" She lifted her eyebrows with the obvious question.

His eyes narrowed and she noted the expression of resentment and also deviousness. "My situation isn't *that* desperate," he said, his posture stiffening with disapproval.

"You must be rather close to the end of the funds I gave you, if you haven't gambled them away already."

"Your scorn is distasteful in a lady. If you show this side to the gentlemen no one will want to enter matrimony with you."

"And that is perfectly desirable," she said. "I have no need to surrender my will, my very life to some tyrannical man who most likely won't have more wits than a flea."

"No man wants a harpy for a wife," he said flatly, his lips curving downward. "You mark my words, there'll be a time when you'll be crawling to me and begging me to marry you."

"I'd rather wed a toad!" she shouted. She walked toward the door of the parlor, wishing she were miles away from Alvin. This house party had started to wear on her, no matter how gracious the Celtborns, and since her cousin had arrived, it had become unbearable.

Her thoughts kept revolving around Sir Richard, and she wondered if he'd made any progress with Laura Endicott. She couldn't get him off her mind, and it wasn't just her obsession with the Ashcroft curse, and Laura's necklace; it was the memory of the man himself that insinuated itself upon her waking hours and in her dreams.

"I don't know how he came to matter in such a way," she said to herself as she marched to her bedchamber. "He's naught but an infuriating male who can't see any farther than his own nose. A pox on all graceless gentlemen."

"Is that you?" her aunt said, peering nearsightedly, as Jill stepped into the room. "I could hear your muttering, and was that a curse you just placed on the entire male species?"

"Yes. . . ." Jill realized the contradiction in her life.

"You're supposed to be dispelling curses, not placing them," Aunt Iddy pointed out.

Jill sighed and sat down on the bed, toying with a silver-backed hairbrush. "Oh, Auntie, why are things so difficult? Sir Richard practically needed a brow-beating before he would agree to help me."

"Brow-beatings are your specialty," Aunt Iddy said with some asperity.

"However dearly I loved Father, he was helpless and useless, and it has been passed on to me to clear up the matters that have weighed down the Ashcrofts for ages. None of my ancestors had the gumption to solve the problems, and that weakness ultimately cost them their lives."

"You can't say that for sure," her aunt replied. "'Tis heresy."

"Be that as it may, we both know the curse exists, and you have watched much of the violence as, one by one, the gentlemen have died."

"And some of the females. My sister—"

"It frightens me to think that something might happen to us, but more than anything it frightens me to think that Alvin would be the last in the line of Ashcrofts. I just can't allow that to happen."

Aunt Iddy pursed her lips, and Jill felt that she agreed even if she actually didn't say the words. They had gone over these grounds many times before.

"Believe you me, Auntie, I will see this to the end, and if only I could find another way, I would never involve Laura Endicott, but she holds the key. I'm certain of that."

"Once this is over, what do you want to do, Jill?"

"I would want to return to Lindenwood, but that's

impossible. We shall travel, or find lodgings by the seaside where I shall read and study."

"Ugh," her aunt replied, giving a visible shiver. "I wish to see you settled, not living a bluestocking life among your books. You have too many opinions as it is, and that trait—"

"You sound just like Alvin," Jill protested. "Next thing you'll say is that no gentleman wants to marry me."

"That sums it up in a nutshell," Aunt Iddy said cruelly. "Most of the time he has more hair than wit, but he's right in this case."

Jill didn't give one whit, but deep in her heart she admitted that her frankness hadn't brought forth a slew of admirers.

Five

"I've received word from Sir Richard," Jill cried two days later as the mail arrived at the Celtborn estate. Aunt Iddy sat ensconced with her embroidery frame and a cup of tea at her elbow in the solarium and she looked expectantly at Jill through her thick glasses. The sun beat down on that part of the house, the golden light reflecting from all the leaves and the marble pillars.

"What does he say?"

"He's convinced Laura to invite us down to Cornwall—as Lady Honoria Iddings and myself as Miss Iddings, to stay at the Endicott Keep for a week, or possibly longer, depending on our success." She danced around the room. "This is the opportunity I've been waiting for, and success is within reach."

"I would not want to count on that until the pendant is in your hand," Aunt Iddy said glumly.

"Don't spoil this. The outcome cannot be anything but successful."

Aunt Iddy looked doubtful, but Jillian would not allow anything to bring her down. The Endicott pendant was within her reach, and she would find a way to appropriate it. With any kind of luck, Laura Endicott might just give it to her.

"Jill, if what you said about the curse is true—"

"Of course it's true!"

"Then it's been in place for centuries, and must be very powerful. You can't just overturn that by making off with an old necklace."

"There's a ritual involved. Father found out what to do and wrote it down, but he was struck down before he could set it into motion."

"Your father, God bless his soul, was a very unworldly fellow and possibly not quite right in the head."

"Aunt Iddy, how can you say that about your own brother-in-law?" Jill berated, outraged. "Father was brilliant, and he understood things that the common man is ignorant about."

"Hocus-pocus," Aunt Iddy replied, two red spots glowing on her cheeks.

Jill knew it was useless speaking of anything connected to her father's work. Aunt Iddy, a staunch traditionalist, simply had no imagination, no "flights of fancy," as she would say with a cynical twist of her lip.

"As I said, the chore sits on my shoulders. I have to see it through," Jill concluded, "there's no one else who cares."

"Or believes," Aunt Iddy added on.

"Great help you are," Jill muttered.

"It's been a long time since I saw the Bodmin Moor." Aunt Iddy stared vaguely into the distance. Jill knew she didn't see well despite the glasses. She needed a new pair.

"We shall take long, vigorous horseback rides and you shall see the gorse and the heather."

"Spare me!" Aunt Iddy fanned herself and looked exhausted at just the thought. "And the heather isn't blooming now, or is it?" She glanced in Jill's direction, an expression of long-suffering on her face. "And I have my hands full with you, dear. There's no telling what kinds of antics you'll stir up."

"Aunt Iddy!"

The older woman sighed. "That's God's truth. I love you dearly, but you're a handful. I wish you would find some decent gentleman and settle down. The responsibility of a fistful of children might anchor you to the ground. 'Twould be a blessing to see you thus occupied."

"No one would want to marry someone of my lineage. The *rumors* you know. So that's another reason why I desire to dispel the curse. I would not want my future husband to be violently struck down in his prime."

Aunt Iddy sighed. "You'd better pursue some more feminine interests if you don't want to linger on the shelf. Moldy books and ancient herbal recipes are not attractive to gentlemen of the *ton,* unless they are scholars as dotty as your father. They are few and far between, thank God."

"So you have told me on numerous occasions, Auntie," Jill said with a tired sigh. She had felt the rejection most keenly in the past, and the only man who had offered for her hand—Alvin—wanted nothing more than her money.

"You are quite pretty in an *unkempt* sort of way. I'm certain there's no fault to find in that area."

"I've never been concerned about the fal-lals of fashion, and I'm unlikely to kindle that kind of interest in the future."

"You might have to if you want to snare a husband," Aunt Iddy replied ominously. "This is your second Season after all."

"Hunting never appealed to me, and I don't believe we should have to resort to manipulative tactics to find me a husband."

"Your inheritance is a great plus."

"Are you saying I'll only find a husband on the strength of my financial background?"

"Since you refuse to do something about that wild black hair and your wardrobe, yes, I'd say your financial situation will be the deciding factor for some gentleman to come up to scratch."

Jill felt like throwing something across the room and punching her pillows, but she only stared at her aunt—her *traitorous* aunt. "Aunt Iddy, I never knew you to be so shallow." She stood, her back stiff with outrage. "I shall take my wild hair and myself off for a ride, and when I return, we shall pack for Cornwall."

Jill hadn't known what to expect of Endicott Keep, but certainly not this gray, grim, and imposing old castle that dwarfed everything that dared to come near. She stared out the coach window as the equipage rolled up the long winding drive.

The witch's ancestors had built this fortress, and you could feel the power in the mighty stones. Jill pictured Laura Endicott as tall and fierce with flashing black eyes and hair that grew to her knees. As the castle loomed over them, an apprehension came over Jill. What if she'd taken on too great a challenge?

She squared her shoulders. No, she would accomplish what she'd come for, no matter how grim or how fearsome the current witch was.

The fresh wind off the sea brought odors of seaweed and fish, and small birds darted and twittered in the oaks scattered around the castle. Clumps of willow grew among boulders that no caretaker had seen fit to remove.

No one had tried to tame the rugged terrain that

marched all the way up to the ancient castle walls, and some groups of planted rose bushes looked forlorn and out of place.

Aunt Iddy's eyes grew very round as she stepped out of the carriage and faced the massive front doors. Her eyes crinkled at the corners as she struggled to focus. "This is a very *large* place, isn't it?"

"The Endicotts are a proud family, I'm sure, but not many members are left of the old line now."

"One could get lost in here and never find one's way out, perhaps even starve to death before anyone could find one," Aunt Iddy said breathlessly.

"Now you're the fanciful one," Jill said scornfully. "A mansion this size will have an army of servants."

A footman, dressed rather simply in a brown homespun suit and no wig, opened the door. No one seemed to care for the niceties of appropriate dress on the backside of Cornwall.

"We are Lady Honoria and Miss Iddings," Jill said imperiously.

He stared at her speculatively, and she regretted that she had to conceal her real identity. Laura would be appalled to know who had just stepped over her threshold. Just the thought made Jill feel like a snake in the grass. She wondered if her shadow was entering long and threatening before her.

"Sir Richard invited us to meet Miss Laura and her family," Aunt Iddy filled in.

He only nodded and let them inside where an elderly butler greeted them in the foyer. Holding broadswords, two rusting suits of armor stood sentinel by the arch that led to the rest of the house. Beyond, Jill could make out massive hand-carved oak furniture and an enormous threadbare Oriental carpet. More suits of armor stood along the walls, and swords and shields of all sizes attached to the paneling spoke of a violent past.

Rapid footsteps echoed along the flagstones, and a young woman dressed in a light blue muslin dress with a lace fichu appeared, a sweet smile on her face. She stood at medium height, slender and graceful. Jill noted a litter of kittens and two small dogs following her, their little claws clicking against the floor. The woman held out both hands toward Jillian. Her clasp felt warm and welcoming.

"I'm Laura Endicott and so pleased to meet you! Richard has spoken so highly of you and how you are old friends of his family. He felt I need some female friends, and he's always right." The last statement she said with a wink.

I'm not the only liar around here, Jill thought ruefully. She'd only known Sir Richard for a week, so old friends they were not. But evidently his word to her could be trusted. He'd been working on her behalf to forward her cause.

"I've been longing to meet some of his friends and family, but I live so secluded here in Cornwall that people are loath to visit. 'Tis the only drawback."

"I think it's a wonderful part of the world to visit," Aunt Iddy said, looking somewhat uncomfortable. She wore a respectable dark brown gown and a fringed shawl, which she pulled closer as if bothered by a chill.

She had complained about the deceit in which she had to be an accomplice, but had resigned herself with a long-suffering sigh when Jill had insisted that it would be the only way to save the Ashcrofts. Aunt Iddy knew there would be no rest until Jill had solved the issue of the Ashcroft curse.

Jill shuddered; there was a definite chill in the air.

"I'm Jillian and this is my aunt Lady Honoria Iddings."

With a brilliant smile, Laura squeezed her hand, and Jill felt a deep stab of guilt because this woman before her was sweetness personified.

Surely, this could not be the descendant of an evil witch. Laura looked more like an angel with her long curly blond hair, rosy complexion, and compassionate eyes. No evil thoughts lived in her mind; 'twas obvious for all to see. The animals evidently adored her as they pawed her for her attention. She ignored them as they tumbled around her feet.

"Welcome to Endicott Keep. I hope you stay for a long time as I'm sorely in need of company. Aunt Penny is a dear, but she spends most of her time embroidering tapestries, an obsession of hers. The current one she started in 1798."

"Ohhh," Aunt Iddy said with reverence in her voice. "A great masterpiece no doubt."

"Yes, you shall see for yourself directly."

"I embroider myself, but my poor eyesight limits my choices in styles and materials."

"You shall have much to talk about with my aunt then," Laura said with another warm smile. "Come along."

Jill's gaze fell on the simple if heavy-looking pendant around Laura's neck and the small hairs on her arms stood on end. Without a doubt this was the Endicott necklace, the key to unlocking the curse that had held the Ashcrofts prisoners for so long. The gray stone seemed to glow with power, but Jill suspected her own imagination created that impression.

Laura gave out nothing but modesty and friendliness. Her dress was made in a slightly outmoded style, and Jill noted the bright blue fabric had faded in the folds, but no one seemed to care.

Jill felt the tightness in her shoulders relax, and knew she could breathe again. Mayhap this woman would be reasonable after all? But what would happen if she revealed her identity to Laura? Would her friendly smile be replaced by one of vengeance?

Torn, Jill felt an urge to confide in this one person who could surely help her, but caution set in. Better tread lightly to see how they progressed.

"Richard mentioned that you were tired of the social whirl, and how glad I am that you decided to come here for a rest. We have plenty of peace."

"What about yourself, have you had a Season in London, Laura?" Jill asked as she gave her pelisse and gloves to the waiting arms of the footman. Smoothing out her canary yellow muslin gown, she checked that their traveling hadn't rumpled the fabric beyond redemption.

Laura shook her head. "No, there has been no need for that. I've been betrothed to Richard for donkey's years." A veil of something came over her beaming face. "I have to confess though that dancing is one of my passions, and we have precious little opportunity to take to the dance floor in these parts."

"Not much of social entertainment?" Aunt Iddy asked, as she made sure her hair still remained in order under her lace-edged cap.

"Now that you're here, we can invite some people and entertain ourselves. We're going to enjoy ourselves." She clapped her hands together as if filled with great anticipation.

Jill realized it didn't take much to amuse Laura. Besides sweetness of character, she had the simplicity of a child. The kittens gamboled around her feet, never far away.

"I will help you to enliven things around here," Jill promised, and surely life would never be the same after she'd obtained the Endicott pendant, but she didn't wish to hurt Laura in any way.

"You sound like a lively person," Laura said with a laugh. "I feel we're going to be great friends."

"I hope so," Jill said, and truly meant it.

Sir Richard entered the room. Jill hadn't heard him coming, but he looked wonderful and virile in a blue riding coat and top boots. His cravat lay in snowy folds at his throat, an elegant contrast to his sun-bronzed skin and dark eyes.

"Richard! You never told me how much I'd like your friends; in fact you've been very close-mouthed, and I'm sorely disappointed in you. How could you not speak in glowing terms about Miss Iddings?"

Red crept above his collar to touch his cheeks. He gave Jill a long, suspicious glance. "I wanted you to find out for yourself, my dear."

"A pleasant surprise indeed." Laura took Jill's arm and led her away as Richard instructed the footmen to carry the luggage up to their rooms.

Aunt Iddy commented in awed tones on the paintings and the architecture as they walked along a hallway to a parlor in the back. From there you could see a view of a sloping lawn and beyond that, jagged black cliffs, and the glittering and wildly blue Irish Sea.

The walls in the room were at least three feet thick, Jill thought, judging by the window casings.

"I would never worry about invasion here," she said and touched the cold stone.

Laura laughed. "In these days, no, but there was a time of chaos and marauding that only these walls know. But at least they are still standing, and perhaps there will one day be more Endicotts to shelter within."

"You're the only one left then?" Jill said.

"'Tis unusual, but yes, I'm the last of my line, but if I have sons, they will continue on."

"A proud family no doubt," Jill said, knowing they had been warriors and illustrious people long ago.

"Certainly." Laura patted a sofa and invited Jill to sit with her. Jill admired the beautiful green brocade curtains with gold fringe, the soft inviting chairs and sofas, and the costly carpet on the floor.

"I ordered tea," Laura said simply.

"Nothing like a bracing cup of tea after a long trip," Aunt Iddy said.

Sir Richard entered the room, and took a stance by the fireplace as if part of the group, but not quite. He had a rather standoffish air, Jill thought, and every glance he threw at her came edged with distrust.

"Richard, I'm surprised you haven't talked about these wonderful people in the past," Laura said reproachfully.

"I haven't had much contact with the ladies until I ran across them at the Celtborns' house party."

At least that was the truth, Jill thought.

"I suspected I could help alleviate your boredom and their exhaustion." As he said the last word, he directed his gaze at Aunt Iddy as if to say he understood that she was tired of squiring Jill around town.

Jill sent him a dagger-sharp look, which he returned with disdain. He had no right to judge her, but it was clear he highly disapproved of her presence.

The two dogs scampered around her feet, and she had to bend down and stroke their silky fur. At least they welcomed her, and in fact, everyone should be grateful that she was here to change history.

"Toby and Bonnie like you," Laura said. "They are very good judges of character, so with their approval, I can safely say that you have a good heart, Jill."

Jill blushed. "Thank you." She eyed the necklace, wondering what it would be like to touch it. She couldn't of course, not today, maybe not tomorrow, but soon.

Footmen rolled in a cart with a tea service and plates of cakes and buns. Jam and clotted cream filled crystal dishes, and a bowl of fruit lent vivid color to the arrangement. The tea, hot and amber, soothed Jill's tired body and mind.

She glanced at two portraits of children and animals on the wall over the fireplace. "Who are they?"

"That's me and my brother James. He died when he was seven, of a fever," Laura explained.

Jill murmured words of sympathy, as she knew how such a loss tore at your heartstrings.

"The keep now belongs to a cousin who lives in the Colonies. I look after it for him."

The door opened anew and an older lady wearing a silk shawl over her outmoded lavender gown stepped inside, peering closely at the group. "Botheration, here you all are." She stepped forward uncertainly, a smile flickering on and off on her face. "I couldn't remember where tea was supposed to be served . . . and could you believe it, I got lost." She shook her white head incredulously and her mouth quivered with distress. "And I've only lived here all my life."

"Aunt Penelope, don't take on so," Laura said kindly. "You know Sir Richard is visiting and he invited some of his friends from London." She introduced Jill and Aunt Iddy. "Aunt Penny is my father's youngest sister."

"Young is a grand exaggeration," Aunt Penny said with a dry laugh. "Mayhap a few decades ago, when powdered hair was all the rage, and skirts billowed like full sails over hoops. Can't say that I miss that kind of fashion."

Aunt Iddy squealed in recognition, and they immediately found a new friend in each other. After many exclamations and fan flutterings the ladies settled down for a coze near the teapot. Laura and Jill exchanged uneasy glances.

"Well," Jill said, "who would've thought they would strike up a friendship that quickly?"

Laura smiled. "It is for us to do the same, don't you think?"

Jill nodded, every moment reminded of the subterfuge she'd brought along with her to the Endicott Keep. If only Laura knew whom she had under her roof, she wouldn't be as willing to share her bread. Jill quickly pushed aside the feeling as she thought of the larger purpose. If it weren't for her, the Ashcroft line would die, but truly, she would see to it that no one would be hurt as she acquired the pendant.

Sir Richard caught her gaze, and his expression reminded her of a thundercloud that was ready to burst over her head. His eyes shot fire, a challenge for her to bring out the truth, and she shrank a little, but then reminded herself of her mission—one that wasn't based on selfishness.

"You would be a huge success in the capital with your fair beauty," she said to Laura, and Sir Richard gave her another thunderous look. It wasn't flattery, by God; she meant every word of it! "The gentlemen would be falling over themselves in their hurry to reach your side."

"Fiddlesticks," Laura said, blushing and clapping her hands to her cheeks.

"In fact, you've been decidedly deprived since you haven't had a chance to do the rounds in London."

"Jillian, not everyone has to spend a Season in London to find a husband."

Only you have to spend several Seasons, Jill read from Sir Richard's expression as he gazed at her. Boorish creature. But she hadn't been desperately looking for a husband. This was only her second Season in Town, and probably her last, as the whirl of activities didn't inspire her much. "Who says that's the sole reason for a lady to attend parties in London?" she challenged him.

"For those who are desperate," he said, evidently joining her to that desperate group of spinsters and young ladies without prospects.

"Yes, you're right of course," Jill said stiffly, "but 'tis rather rude to speak about it—as if you're above that kind of situation and proud of it."

"That's a slanderous statement, Miss Iddings. You make me into a snob."

"You took the words into your mouth, Sir Richard. In other words, you started this conversation, not I."

Laura looked round-eyed from one to the other. "You're bickering like children in the schoolroom. Either you're comfortable with the banter, or you can't stand each other. I hope my premier theory is correct."

Jill didn't want to argue, and she felt guilty about crossing swords with Sir Richard, but ever since she'd laid eyes on him here at the Keep, he'd been rubbing her the wrong way. "We're only bandying words about, Laura. 'Tis still my firm opinion that you would be a raging success."

Laura bent down to pet one of the dogs at her feet. "I don't need the social whirl as I keep myself wholly occupied with my animals. They are the best companions, aren't they? You never hear them argue or speak derogatorily in any way, nor do they judge you."

Jill nodded and envied her innocence. "Yes, they have all the admirable qualities, so unlike mankind."

"You sound very cynical for your age," Penelope Endicott said suddenly, breaking off her own conversation with Aunt Iddy.

"When you have to fend for yourself, you learn the ways of the world," Jill replied. "My family has been criticized at length for some of their 'oddities' as they might be perceived, and I learned early on to protect myself, and sometimes my father."

She realized she skirted the abyss by bringing up her family as Laura was bound to start asking questions, and then she might have to lie again. Oh, drat! Why had she opened her big mouth? She just couldn't lie any more as it went against every fiber of her being.

She continued before Laura could open her mouth. "'Tis a pity you don't have a brother who might take you around, Laura."

"A brother, or a sister would've been a great comfort, but I remained alone. Truth is, my mother lacked strength. I doubt she could've given me any siblings even if she'd wanted to."

Jill tasted one of the iced cakes, relishing its melting sweetness. "I have only one cousin, and he's a great nuisance." At least that was the truth.

"What of your parents?"

"They have passed on to their rewards," Jill said,

feeling a stab of longing for her father. If it weren't for Aunt Iddy, she would be very much alone.

"Have you noticed that our backgrounds are similar?" Laura asked. "We have no family to speak of."

Jill met Sir Richard's gaze, noting the warning light. She sensed his anger at the deception, but at least he was holding up his end of the bargain. She wondered for how long, and she prayed the matter of the curse could be taken care of without delay.

She glanced at the coveted rock at the base of Laura's throat and felt Sir Richard's gaze burn through her, but she refused to look at him or respond to his anger.

Since he'd committed himself this deeply he would have to see the mission through.

Six

The next morning after Jill had bathed in a hipbath in her room, donned a fresh morning gown of light blue sarcenet, and fastened a lace fichu at her throat, she almost collided with Laura in the hallway.

"I was so excited last night I couldn't sleep. How wonderful to have found a new friend," Laura cried, beaming. "My life has been brightened by your appearance on my doorstep and I'm immensely grateful to Richard for having brought you." She pulled Jill's arm gently. "Come, I'll show you my chamber."

At the end of the hallway, she opened the door to a large airy bedroom with pillow seats on the wide stone casements of the windows, and a magnificent view of the sea. On every chair and on the four-poster mahogany bed rested cats, and in a basket on the floor scrambled a litter of tiny puppies. Laura pointed at them. "My new wards."

"I've noticed that you have an amazing rapport with your four-legged friends."

"Yes, but that's neither here nor there." Laura pulled Jill to the window and pointed across the hills to some chimneystacks that protruded above a copse of trees. "Do you see that mansion?"

"Yes . . . what little there is to see."

"It's the Sandhurst estate—Julian Temple, Viscount Sandhurst. Have you ever been introduced?"

Jill thought for a moment. "The name sounds familiar to me, but for some reason, I can't put a face with the name. I doubt we move in the same circles."

Laura smiled, somewhat secretively, Jill thought. "He has a handsome face at that. I've known Julian all my life." The smile disappeared and she eyed Jill speculatively. "He is not married, and I believe you might be a possible candidate for his wife. That way, we could always live near each other."

Jill spread out her hands in a gesture of helplessness. "You've only known me for one day, Laura."

"Yes, but I trust my instincts on this matter."

You're an innocent and I'm the last person you should trust, Jill thought. "It's no secret that I'm looking for a husband, but more to please Aunt Iddy than myself. I don't have a desire to marry anyone."

"Until you meet the right gentleman. Julian cuts quite a dash, and he has a respectable fortune to keep you in all the comforts."

Jill felt frustrated and guilty. "I appreciate your thoughtfulness, but surely—"

"I shall invite him to dinner tonight," Laura interrupted with glee. "And you shall see for yourself. I think you'll be madly enamored before the week is out."

"One thing I do admire in you is your optimism, Laura."

"Flummery. You must be interested in meeting someone who might be a good candidate for matrimony."

"You already have me married off to this neighbor of yours?" Jill said incredulously. "As I pointed out, I'm not desperate to wed anyone."

"Desperation has nothing to do with it. It may be the road to True and Undying Love."

Jill could not shake the uneasy feeling of her deceit, as Laura wanted nothing more than to make her happy. "Are you looking forward to your own nuptials? Sir Richard is a gentleman and quite dashing in his own way."

"Richard is all that a woman would want, thoughtful, responsible, even-tempered, but he's rather a starched shirt, don't you think?"

Jill silently agreed. "That's easier to live with than a gamester or a rake. At least you know Sir Richard is honorable. He does have a lot of energy even if he's a stick-in-the-mud."

"Mayhap if he let go of his principles somewhat, he would improve." Laura sighed. "And then there's the loss of his sister. He's not been the same since."

"Granted it's a heavy burden, but he won't remain in that state forever." She patted Laura's hand. "I think you're fortunate to have his pledge."

Laura smiled but the smile didn't quite reach her eyes. "My father and his father were close at one time. Not that I knew either one of them, but they made sure I'll be taken care of, and for that I am grateful." She plopped down on one of the window seats and a gray tabby jumped up into her lap, arching its back and purring. "Emmy here is grateful too as she knows that as I'm well taken care of, she will always have a warm place to sleep."

"That's always a positive way of looking at it. You have such a sunny disposition."

Jill found that she was already growing very fond of her new friend. If only the matter of the pendant didn't hang between them, things would be so much easier. She sat down next to Laura on the cushion. A salt-laden breeze blew in from the sea through the open window. All this time when Laura had been speaking, Jill had stared at the Endicott pendant. It looked dull and rather ugly in the bright morning light, but it held a certain something that commanded attention.

"Life is simple and peaceful here. One of my favorite things is to lie flat on my back in the grass and look at the cloud formations in the sky. They have whole stories to tell. And everywhere around me there are flowers. I so enjoy their nodding in the breeze—and the birds singing everywhere."

"I share those simple pleasures." She almost slipped and mentioned the beauty and serenity of Lindenwood, which would've brought horror to Laura's eyes rather than the smile that lingered there. She took a deep breath and indicated the Endicott pendant with her hand. "That is a curious piece. Is it old?"

"I'm astounded. No one has ever shown any interest in this stone, and now everyone seems to notice. First Richard, and now you." Laura fingered the pendant on its worn chain. "'Tis old, centuries in fact, but I like it in its plainness. It gives me comfort, as if telling me that I'm connected to my ancestors in a most ancient and powerful way. I never take it off, you know, excepting when I bathe."

Distressed, Jill let the words sink in and wondered if she would have to simply steal it at some point. The thought went against her grain completely, and a quiet desperation began to fill her. Her mission was turning out to be extraordinarily difficult by the looks of it.

"I wouldn't mind having a pendant like that," Jill said with a dash of hope that Laura in her kindheartedness would just simply give it to her.

But Laura didn't move to take it off. "Yes . . . I understand that, but there's only one. I don't know if you could ever find another. I believe it was carved in far off lands, where, I'm not sure. Possibly it's Norse or Egyptian."

Jill nodded. "You're right, there would not be one like it—it's original—but perhaps a replica."

Laura nodded. "Something similar could certainly be fashioned, and might've been, but it wouldn't be quite the same."

"It would not carry the weight of the ages." Or the curse, Jill thought. She reached out to touch it, but couldn't quite make herself do it. Laura looked at her curiously.

"Would you mind if I were to look at it more closely? You've awakened my curiosity."

Laura still didn't make an effort to take it off. Jill knew she never would.

Laura said, "My mother always cautioned me to keep it close; why I'm not so sure, but she claimed it held the power of our ancestors, and I rather like the idea of that connection as I am quite alone except for Aunt Penny."

"She's a dear, but I find that aunts tend to be busy-bodies in a well-meaning way, and they have usually their own *firm* opinion, which has to be shared at all times."

"Aunt Penny is rather unassuming. She lives in her own mind, creating worlds on tapestries."

"Aunt Iddy is too blind to embroider much even if she said she does, but she enjoys walks and long talks with friends, and lots and lots of tea."

"Oh, yes."

They shared a laugh at the idiosyncrasies of their relatives, finding yet another part of their lives that they shared.

"We could easily have been sisters," Laura said, squeezing Jill's hand.

Jill gently extracted her hand, knowing she shouldn't let herself be touched by affection, or she wouldn't be able to accomplish her mission. Nothing, *nothing* could stand in her way!

"Mother would've liked you, Jill."

"Tell me about her."

"She was poorly a lot of the time, and she kept much to herself. Never one to talk much—not at all like myself. I must take after Father's side of the family." She thought for a moment. "My mother loved to read and had a great store of knowledge, some of it ancient. If she'd been a man, she would've been educated, but in her own quiet way she knew as much as the teachers at Oxford. She enjoyed history and the arts. She knew everything about Greek architecture and Sumerian potions."

"Sumerian potions?"

"Sumeria is a land that existed before history near Syria and Persia, as far as I know. They knew how to use herbs in healing ways, and she had old accounts for potions that would cure any kind of pain or illness. She kept that part very quiet, as she didn't want to be labeled a witch. My mother was a stickler for propriety, so it still surprises me to think that her interests were that varied, but she rarely spoke to me about them, and I've learned nothing about potions."

Jill so wanted to tell her about her father, but she couldn't find the words to describe his dedicated studies of ancient truths and forgotten remedies. "'Tis rather odd she didn't pass on her knowledge."

"I found some books after she passed on, and I've been studying about herbs. In fact, I've tried some on the animals with very good effect."

"Perhaps everything was put on paper in the old tomes that your mother left behind. Next thing we know, you'll be putting spells on everyone to try them out." Jill purposely made her voice light and airy.

"Never!" Laura looked outraged. "I would never resort to something that underhanded. I very much doubt Mother dabbled in anything magic except the herbs. She would not allow some heathen knowledge to cross our threshold."

Mrs. Endicott would turn in her grave if only she knew what was happening, Jill thought. "Yes, of course. Would you mind showing me some of those old tomes?"

"Not at all. They will make good bedtime reading for you while you're here."

"I've always been interested in history because in it lies our roots, and family history is important."

"I'm delighted that you take any kind of interest in things that have been passed down through my family. It shows your dedication." She looked thoughtful. "I ought to learn more about yours, too."

"Oh no," Jill blurted out, startled.

"Why not? You take kindly interest in me—"

"We don't have such an illustrious past, rather boring in fact."

"I doubt that anything about you is boring, Jill. You are full of *joie de vivre* and that comes from somewhere in the family."

"I spent a great deal of time alone, or with Aunt Iddy. I was never reared for a place in polite society, and I don't care a fig for how people perceive me or whether they accept my opinions or not."

"I would never dare to act in a rebellious fashion," Laura said quietly.

Jill laughed. "Some biddy called me a 'shocking minx' and predicted that I would never find a husband unless I changed my ways. She possibly envied the fact that I don't have to find someone to sustain me financially. She has five daughters to marry off, and they don't have a feather to fly with, only an illustrious name."

"I am appalled that someone would criticize you in such a way."

"Bah, I'm not afraid of someone's careless words."

Laura pulled Jill to her feet. "Let's go downstairs and fortify ourselves with some coffee, and mayhap you care to go riding with me later on the moor."

"That would be a pleasure. The breeze from the sea is always invigorating."

They had breakfast in the gloomy dining hall where more suits of armor, shields, and grim swords showed order within the thick stone walls and reminded everyone to behave.

Penelope noticed Jill's scrutiny of the old rusting armor. "Gives me indigestion every time I eat here," the older woman said. "It's as if eyes stare at you through those slits in the helmets."

"You're being fanciful, Aunt Penny," Laura said with a laugh. She served herself from the sideboard, fare like smoked ham, kippers and eggs, and crispy bacon. The delicious smells made Jill's stomach squeeze with hunger. She met Aunt Penny's welcoming smile and a wave of guilt overcame her. Her mission would be so much easier to accomplish if the Endicotts treated her with less kindness, but Laura was graciousness personified.

How was it ever possible that she had descended from Lucinda the Evil? That Laura had angelic qualities was obvious to see. Whatever dark Lucinda had passed on to the Endicotts, it hadn't affected Laura.

Innocents tended to be protected, as they could see no evil in others. The knowledge plagued Jill. How could she steal something from an innocent? She would forever burn in some unpleasant place, wouldn't she? It didn't matter how pure her motives were.

She served herself some kippers and eggs, but it was hard to swallow the guilt sitting like a stone in her middle.

Brumley poured coffee from a shining silver pot, and the warmth of the liquid fortified her. With some food in her stomach she felt stronger, ready to face the world. The first challenge was Sir Richard as he walked into the room.

"Richard! You are about early this morning. Did you have a pleasant rest at The Duck and Arrow?"

For propriety's sake, Sir Richard stayed at the local inn, but he spent most of his time at the Keep. He looked attractive in an immaculate coat, striped waistcoat, and a flawless neck cloth. Unfortunately, his dour expression marred the picture of perfection.

"Good morning," he greeted everyone with a stiff bow. He bent over Laura and kissed her on the cheek. "Thank you for enquiring. The Duck and Arrow has everything you can wish for except comfortable beds, but I'm not here to complain," he added smoothly.

He avoided Jill's gaze, his attention going to the covered silver dishes on the sideboard.

"Please join us," Laura said, patting the chair beside her.

"I already broke my fast, but after a brisk ride, something warm would be just the thing." He walked to the sideboard, and Jill wondered if she would have a chance to speak with him about the pendant. There was no doubt that she would need his help, and she suspected it would be an uphill battle from now on. He seemed most reluctant, outright ornery.

She followed him under the pretext to collect

some more food. He eyed her narrowly as if sensing her purpose to speak with him, and gave her no encouragement.

Aloud, she spoke, "Endicott Keep is a most imposing place, and I'm so grateful that you invited us here, Sir Richard. In all honesty, I've never met such gracious hosts."

"Flattery won't work," he said *sotto voce*. "I suspected you would enjoy a sojourn here," he added aloud.

"I need your help," she whispered under her breath. "Laura refuses to take off her pendant even for a moment."

"I don't blame her. She's probably smelling a rat, a very big rat," he replied coldly as he politely scooped egg onto her plate. "And she'll send one of her most trusted mousers after it."

"You are not very helpful, Sir Richard, and scolding me is useless. I've come this far and I won't give up now. This is the best opportunity I'll ever have for ending the misfortunes of the Ashcrofts."

He groaned softly. "Why did I ever let myself be pulled into your wicked schemes?"

"Because at some point you realized the importance of my mission."

"What are you two whispering about?" Laura demanded to know from the table.

"We're commenting on the wonderful quality of the food," Jill said hurriedly.

"Liar," he said between his teeth.

"Yes, I am," she freely admitted.

"It's nothing to be proud of."

"Who says I'm proud of it?" Jill brought her plate back to the table and sat down, swallowing her ire with difficulty. She gave Laura a forced smile. "Your cook has a divine touch with eggs."

Laura nodded. "I always thought Marcel was wasted here in the country when he could've made a huge success in London, but he's happy to stay here. Says the sea air is good for his lungs. I shall test his mettle with a dinner party in your honor, Jill, to see if he's still capable of serving up a feast."

"I have no doubt about that," Jill replied.

Sir Richard sat down next to his fiancée and spread his napkin across his lap. "We have yet to celebrate our engagement," he said. "I'd like to send a notice to the papers and invite some of my family and friends."

"But Richard, we have been engaged for *ages*. I don't see why we have to do something—"

"To let the world know of course," he said coolly. "We are going about this in style, you know. Even if we won't have a grand ceremony, we want to do it right."

Laura nodded, her demeanor very quiet. Jill wondered if she worried about living with a gentleman; Laura definitely had a shy side, but she seemed comfortable enough with Sir Richard. "If I ever were to be betrothed, I would like a large gathering to celebrate my new status. After all, it is the beginning of a new life."

"Yes . . . you are right, Jill. I'm just not used to the idea of being the center of attention."

"You will get used to it," Sir Richard said firmly. "I'm not one to do things by half measure."

I shall make you eat those words if you don't help me with the pendant, Jill thought. That would force him to bring forth some results. "That's good to know," she said out loud.

"I know you're not, Richard. Perhaps if you weren't so . . . so perfect. . . ." Laura's words trailed off, and Jill wondered at such a comment coming from her new friend.

Sir Richard chuckled and raised his eyebrows in a question. "Should I interpret that as an insult, or——?"

"I didn't mean to imply anything. You're kind and dependable, and so very respectable——"

Jill filled in the rest silently for Laura "and so very boring." Evidently Laura had a soft spot for the wilder sort of gentleman. She would be one who swooned over the romanticism of a gallant highwayman as he robbed her of all her jewelry. Ah! That was a thought. If things became desperate, there would always be that possibility of acquiring the pendant. But that would be going to a ridiculous length to achieve her goals.

Oh, how that pendant mocked her even now! It lay dully against Laura's fair skin as if safe in its knowledge that it was untouchable. Perhaps if she were fortunate the clasp would break on the chain. Her thoughts traveled in impossible circles, never at peace. She wondered if she would ever experience peace in her life.

"Respectable—me?" Sir Richard commented.

Laura clapped her hand to her mouth and blushed fiercely.

"Now I'm beginning to take your statements as insults." He looked somewhat uncomfortable as Aunt Iddy peered at him nearsightedly through her thick glasses.

"I didn't mean——"

"Respectable and dependable are the two most beautiful traits in a gentleman," the older woman said. "Trust me. Ramshackle here-and-therians won't cause you anything but grief."

"I have known many a selfish oaf in my lifetime," Aunt Penny said. "They think of no one but themselves."

Jill thought of her cousin, a good example of the selfish oaf.

"I was courted by a gentleman in my youth who preened in every mirror we passed and in every window." Aunt Penny continued. "I realized right then and there that I would always be secondary in his life. Very handsome fellow he was, and so popular with the young ladies. He had a charm that eeled its oily ways into your graces, but I saw him for what he was before it was too late."

"Is that why you never married?" Jill asked.

Aunt Penny dabbed a lace-edged handkerchief at her eyes. "I was betrothed once, but he was lost at sea in a storm as he sailed from the West Indies where his family owned a plantation."

"I'm sorry," Jill and Aunt Iddy said in unison.

"I've only loved once, and never met another gentleman who interested me in that way, and then I found myself firmly on the shelf."

"A most uncomfortable position, I assume," Sir Richard said, cutting up his ham into small pieces.

Aunt Penny shook her head. "No, not at all. No one has dictated my life since my father died, and it has been nothing but blessing after blessing."

"'Tis clear you have a rather negative disposition toward the male species—if you don't mind me saying so," Sir Richard added crisply.

"In what way?" Jill challenged. "All I've heard here on this matter, I've experienced as well."

Sir Richard lifted his eyebrows. "That we're vain and self-serving?" He gave an incredulous laugh. "Come now, you can't judge everyone from the viewpoint of one disappointment or two."

"It matches remarkably with Miss Endicott's observation, so there must be some truth to it."

Sir Richard wiped his mouth with a crisp napkin. "I know that I'm sorely outnumbered here, and it's not fair that I should have to be the object of your scorn."

"I agree with you," Laura said in heated defense. "Everyone experiences disappointment at times, but that doesn't mean every gentleman has to be tarred and feathered."

"Dear," Aunt Penny said, "you just have to remember that you haven't had much experience as you've been living very sheltered all of your life."

"I believe I'll never have to endure such disappointment," Laura said and patted Sir Richard's arm. She gave him a beseeching glance. "You would never fail me, would you?"

How anyone could ever fail those puppy eyes was inconceivable, Jill thought.

Sir Richard looked uncomfortable. "I should hope not, my dear. I'm sure I have my faults, but shallow selfishness is not one of them. You can't be selfish and take care of younger people—not if you want to do it properly."

"How are your young wards?"

"They are growing up quickly. They are well accomplished and I'm very proud of them. Miss Hampton, my aunt, takes very good care of them, and I learned the word 'responsibility' from a young age."

That's why you are so stuffy, Jill wanted to shout, but she primly set down her fork and folded her napkin. She sensed his gaze on her in a silent challenge. She returned his look, and said, "Sometimes growing up too soon makes us more serious than if we had a more lenient youth."

"More dull and boring, you mean?" His voice had the edge of broken glass.

"You jumped to that conclusion all by yourself," she evaded deftly.

Laura cleared her throat delicately. "I'm sure Jill would never consider you boring, Richard. In my experience, dull people have their attention absorbed in ancient tomes at all times. They have no concept about the world around them, but you Richard, are the most worldly gentleman I've met besides Julian."

"All two of us?" Richard chided gently.

Laura laughed and nodded. "That's right." She glanced at Jill. "I'm certain that Jill has a lot more knowledge."

"And a much more disparaging view," Richard filled in, his voice tinged with censure.

Laura set down her cup firmly as Jill opened her mouth to respond. Clearly she had no patience for further confrontation. "Let's take that morning ride, why don't we?" she suggested with an unexpectedly commanding glance at Jill.

Jill nodded mutely and rose from the table. "With great pleasure."

Seven

The morning air felt crisp and clear against Jill's face as she and Laura rode through the spinney on the south side of the estate and out toward the moor. The stable groom had saddled a spirited mare for her, and she enjoyed the horse's enthusiasm at being able to stretch her legs.

Her moss green riding habit with its matching hat and gold frog closings felt too tight and confining, and she wished she could just toss convention to the winds and fling off her jacket. But it would surely shock her friend. It was too early in the relationship to shock anyone, she thought.

Laura looked appealing in her rose velvet outfit that had seen better days, but why bother with elegant fashions in a remote spot like the Keep? No one present except the servants to admire her, bless her soul.

The gently rounded contours of the endless moor stretched out before them, gorse and heather abundant underfoot. Curlew and swallow wheeled high above their heads, jubilant bird song permeating the air.

Rarely did you hear birds bicker in the heated fashion of humans when they wanted to have their point accepted as the only true one. "Oh, why does he have to be right all the time?" she cried to the moor.

Laura was riding ahead of her, but her words must've carried on the wind. She turned around in the saddle, and yelled, "Sir Richard?"

"Oh, anyone," Jill replied irately. "I do seem to cross swords with gentlemen habitually and—him—endlessly."

"That is because you're both proud. He does not want to be bested by a mere female, and you . . . well, you would find it difficult to bend to a male."

Jill frowned. "Why, you're very perceptive."

"Therein lies your strength and your weakness," Laura said simply and Jill didn't sense criticism, only goodwill from her new friend. "No man will be able to take you for granted."

"You're right, but I hope I'm only unbending where there's a need to be firm."

"That's strength tempered with wisdom." Laura laughed and pointed to the winding path. "Let's race."

"With pleasure!"

Jill saw the narrow lane among the heather and gave her mare free rein. The horse flew along the path, clumps of dirt and grass flying. The wind tore at Jill's hat, and loosened her chignon. Before she knew it, her dark tresses flew down her back and her hat hung from its green, knotted ribbons.

Her foul mood lifted as she enjoyed the speed and the power of the mount beneath her. What Sir Richard thought of her mattered not one iota. Once her mission was accomplished, she would never have to deal with him again.

Sir Richard paced the old gallery upstairs at the Keep, and gave the stiff old portraits an occasional stare. Laura's father looked down on him with a perpetual expression of disapproval.

"Dash it all! I didn't have much choice, did I?" Sir Richard said angrily to the painting. "Jill pushed and pushed, and now look where we are, in a full-blown deception, something I cannot abide."

Lionel Endicott frowned, his eyebrows beetled gray tufts that held a certain menace.

"I don't know how Jillian managed to convince me to take part in her game." He rubbed his neck in frustration. "How could I ever have been fooled into believing her insane story about the Ashcroft curse? That woman has windmills in her head, and I can't believe my own stupidity." He glanced around at the empty corridor and made a groan of frustration. "She's made me so desperate I'm talking to myself now. How could I let myself sink so low?" He made another sound of frustration, but no one on the walls seemed to care about his dilemma. They all glowered, mouths pinched thin.

He stared at Lionel Endicott wondering how his father could've had a lifelong friendship with this unforgiving and sour-looking man. The painter had done nothing to soften the harsh planes of his face, and Sir Richard wondered how Lionel could've fathered such a sweet daughter. Laura must be taking after her mother's side of the family.

Her mother's portrait had softness, a hint of a smile, and small dogs rested at her feet. Perhaps Laura's knack with animals came from her mother.

Major deception was no way to start out a new life. He racked his brain to think of ways to get rid of Jillian, but he knew she would never give up and leave without the Endicott pendant, as she firmly believed in the damned curse.

Clearly there were some serious flaws in her upbringing.

The ugly fact that she would not leave without the pendant faced him ruthlessly. *He had invited her to the Keep!* What in the world had induced him to do so? Jillian's undeniable charms? Her power of persuasion? His fear of the scandal involving his sister becoming public?

The situation with Laura had not been as real as it was today; she had seemed to be someone distant without importance even though she would soon be his bride. He should've spent more time to get to know her, and then he wouldn't be in this sort of pickle.

He cursed the day he'd laid eyes on Jillian Ashcroft. "Devil take it, how do I solve this problem?"

Jillian wasn't much concerned about such dark and angry thoughts thrown her way. She wholly enjoyed the ride and the company. For one glorious hour she forgot about the Endicott pendant, and just enjoyed the freedom of the moor. She reined in on a small knoll and looked in all directions. To the West, she could still see the silver glitter of the sea; to the North the crenellated towers of the Keep. The gentle wind played in her hair, and the air smelled of the earth the horses had kicked up.

"This is more beautiful than I could ever imagine," she cried as the breeze batted strands of hair across her face. She tried to bring some semblance of order to her tresses, but they refused to cooperate.

"I pray that you'll be a guest here often," Laura said. "Once I marry Sir Richard, we'll invite more people to the Keep I'm sure. He has many friends, but I haven't met any of them except you."

"You've decided to live here then and not at Eversley?"

Laura made a *moue*. "To be honest, we haven't spoken of that as yet."

"Evidently you haven't spoken much with Sir Richard as it is."

Laura shook her head, gripping the reins tightly as her mare wanted to dance away. "No . . . he's just started to spend more time with me. Before that he was practically a stranger, except for what I learned through his correspondence."

"He appears to know what he wants, but he doesn't speak to you about it; I would find that highly frustrating. I would want to know everything about my future husband."

Laura nodded. "He's being more talkative this time. Mayhap he's getting used to the idea of marrying me. It was forced upon us, but I don't think it's a bad solution."

Jill agreed. "He's a good man. I believe he's struggled to keep Eversley afloat, and he wouldn't want you to think that he's only marrying you for your money." Jill sensed the truth of that in her heart.

They heard a shout behind them, and as they turned in their saddles, they saw a young gentleman riding up on a great tawny gelding. Accompanying him was another, younger man.

"Julian!" Laura cried with obvious delight. "And Edgar."

The men slowed down their mounts, dust billowing away as the hooves came to a halt. The gelding pawed the ground and snorted, and Jill's mare took offense, bucking. Jill clamped her leg more firmly around the horn of the sidesaddle to prevent a fall, and the mare quieted down.

Laura introduced the two gentlemen who swept off their hats gallantly. "I spoke to you about Julian, and Edgar Brodhill is his nephew. His older sister lives in Scotland. Edgar is down from Cambridge."

"A pleasure to meet you, Miss Iddings," Julian said with a smile that could've melted a heart of stone. "Miss Laura spoke of your arrival, and I'm pleased that she finally is becoming more connected to society."

His eyes sparkled with mischief and crinkled at the corners as he gave her another dazzling smile. The wind blew his wavy brown hair beguilingly across his forehead, and there was no woman on earth who would be left untouched by such charm, Jill thought, feeling a vague sense of suspicion.

He was *too* perfect somehow, but she couldn't exactly place her own sense of uneasiness. Too handsome men made her suspicious automatically as she mistrusted their motives. She hoped her instincts were wrong in this case as it was obvious that Laura was very fond of the man.

Julian toyed with Laura's hand as their horses stood closely together. They appeared to have an unspoken conversation with their eyes.

"All this fresh air makes me bilious," Edgar said in a peevish voice. His starched shirt points rose so high he could barely move his head, a detail that made him look terribly self-important. His hair, or the little that could be seen under the curled rim of his hat, was sandy in color and coaxed and pomaded into the latest fashion. This obviously was no country bumpkin.

"Come now, Nevvy, a little fresh air never hurt anyone. You've been too involved with your books, and all it will give you is nearsightedness and a stooped back."

"Books?" Edgar looked surprised, and Jill suspected his repulsion to fresh air fell in with the smoky and damp air he breathed regularly in gambling dens and wine cellars. She was sure Edgar did not have an intimate relationship with his academic books.

His brown gaze swept down his nose and over her form, taking in her wayward hair. She immediately sensed his disapproval, but she didn't follow her impulse to do something about the untidy mass. She returned his gaze with great hauteur. The man acted like a yokel.

"I daresay Mr. Brodhill puts his studies before all else," Jill said. "Education will make a man—without it, he's as ignorant as the common chimney sweep."

Edgar stiffened noticeably, and his cheeks took on a tint of red. "'Pon rep—"

Julian laughed, clearly unaware of the tension in the air. "Ah! Do I detect an educated female?"

"A bluestocking, you mean?" Jill fumed in silence.

"You mentioned that word, not I," he replied smoothly. "In fact, I prefer ladies with some semblance of wit. Insipid and ingratiating misses and blatant husband hunters make me ride off posthaste."

"I could see that, Lord Sandhurst. Heaven forfend that you would have to face a commitment to some insipid miss, or one that swoons at the sight of an ant."

Under her breath she said she'd pray for any miss who would be foolish enough to fall for the viscount's charms, as he would never make an offer for her unless she came with a fortune. But like so many of the eligible bachelors, he would probably want his precious blood propagated at some point, and most likely his bride would be someone he could easily dominate.

Laura would be appalled if she knew my thoughts, Jill suspected, but unfortunately it was too easy to read people's character. Her judgment may have been a tiny bit harsh, but she would never voice it aloud.

Julian laughed, but she saw a flash of ice in his eyes. "Your friend has great wit, Laura."

"Jill is rather forthright and I suspect used to people who speak their mind," Laura said pleasantly. "She's most courageous. Julian, what are you doing out this early? Usually I don't see you until later in the day."

"We came from Pendenny this morning. Attended a card party at the home of one of my cronies, and we were late leaving."

Laura's smile faltered. "I see . . . you must be very tired."

"Not so much that I can't enjoy a beautiful morning, and a chat with two enchanting ladies," he replied, his charm full-blown.

"Julian, you're such a rogue!" Laura paused and glanced at Jill as if thinking hard. She addressed Julian anew. "Would you and Edgar like to come to dinner tonight? We dine at six."

"Six? Such country hours," Edgar commented spitefully.

"I'd be delighted, and so would Edgar, wouldn't you?" He turned to the younger man who nodded noncommittally, his nose very high in the air.

They bowed in their saddles, tipped their hats once more, and then tore off down the path in a cloud of dust.

"Isn't he beautiful, Jill?" Laura said with a wistful lilt in her voice.

"Indeed he is, but he strikes me as a man attached to his freedom, and perhaps attached to his own pleasures. Does he have time for anyone else?"

Laura looked down. "I don't know. He has always been careful about his freedom. Julian dreamed of traveling, y'see, but the burden of his inheritance fell on his shoulders when his cousin passed away."

"It must've been a hard blow for him," Jill said, pressing her tongue firmly into her cheek.

"Julian is the most wildly romantic figure in these parts. His escapades are legend, and his *joie de vivre* is infectious. He quite lifts my spirits when I see him."

Jill stared at her friend closely. "I pray you're not enamored of him?"

Laura reddened, but shook her head. "I was when very young and foolish . . . but no longer. There would never be any hope of a union with Julian. Besides I know all about his adventures, because he tells me, just like he would a favorite confidante. They are appalling of course, so I blush to think that I would in any way involve myself with him."

"I'm not missish, but I suspect it's highly inappropriate that Lord Sandhurst would confide in you, an unwed, inexperienced lady."

Laura shrugged. "I'm not shocked. Julian is Julian, and I understand him well. Nothing he does ever shocks me. We get along splendidly."

"I suppose that when you truly know someone, it becomes that way. You don't judge him."

Laura looked after the two men who diminished with every yard of moor they crossed. Our four-legged friends don't judge us, so I try to take the same attitude toward people. 'Tis not always easy."

Jill nodded. "'Tis difficult indeed, but you're nobler than I." There must be an error along the blood-lines from Lucinda the Evil, she thought. Laura has not one ounce of wickedness inside and Jill guessed that she would not uphold any kind of grudge against the Ashcrofts. But that had yet to be seen.

Eight

The dinner party started with a glass of sherry in the front parlor. Even here, a few suits of armor guarded the room. Jill reminded herself that she had to count the suits when she had some time to spare. Illustrious warriors had fought their battles and their iron protection, some very intricately wrought, had been collected, cared for, and displayed over the centuries.

Tapestries and lit candles in iron candelabra also lent color and interest to the room, whose small windows prevented an infusion of light.

Aunt Penny and Aunt Iddy sat on chairs, fine gowns of lavender and gray silk spread delicately around them. Aunt Penny looked beautiful in lavender against her white hair, and Aunt Iddy had never been one for strong colors.

"I daresay it was a trying day with so much to prepare," Aunt Penny said to Laura.

"Not at all. 'Twas all very exciting," Laura replied.

"I had to resort to smelling salts to stave off my agitation over so many comings and goings from the kitchen," the aunt said crankily. Even now she waved the small crystal bottle under her nose.

Aunt Iddy's face held a staunch expression. She'd seen livelier situations unfold.

Jill glanced down at her own royal blue silk gown with white lace along the hem, wrists, and neckline.

Pearls adorned her ears and her throat, and her hair had been tamed and put up by her maid in a becoming chignon touched here and there with tiny silk flowers.

Laura looked lovely in a simple straight gown of aquamarine silk shot with silver threads. She clung to Sir Richard's arm and laughed at something he was whispering in her ear.

A wave of jealousy overcame Jillian as she stared at them, and the feeling unsettled her no end. Surely she had absolutely no reason to be attached to Sir Richard in any way other than business.

That was all, but her heart had started pounding the moment she saw his handsome form dressed in a black evening coat and breeches. He looked so remote and serious, but obviously he could joke with his fiancée.

A fire leaped and bounced in the grate, and Jill was grateful for the warmth as the stone walls held no heat at all from the sun. She stood with her back to the gentle flames, and the sherry also warmed her inside.

Sir Richard stood at her side, and when she turned to glance in his direction, he looked back at her. A current sizzled between them, and her breath caught in her throat.

There was something so annoying about him, but also something so wildly attractive. She didn't know where to look as discomfort took hold of her usually confident disposition.

Laura left his side to greet Julian and Edgar at the door. She pulled them to the armchairs where the two older ladies sipped their wine and engaged them in conversation. Jill took the opportunity to speak with Sir Richard even if she felt very reluctant to do so. Any conversation with him at this point would be very difficult.

"Laura is a wonderful hostess," she said lamely.

He nodded. "She's graciousness personified, and she *means* it. There's nothing underhanded or calculating within her. I doubt she even knows the words."

Jill was well aware of the cynicism in his voice. "Yes, she's an innocent. Maybe living a sheltered life like this does that to a person."

He shook his head. "It's all in *her*, not in her surroundings, though life here is not exactly a 'den of iniquity.'"

She couldn't help but laugh, and she swallowed a sip of sherry the wrong way. Coughing delicately, she turned toward the fire so as not to draw attention to herself.

"Are you choking to death?" He gently slapped her back, and his touch set her heart racing.

She shook her head and straightened her back. "You wish."

"No, I don't wish," he said forcefully, in a low voice. "I only wish I'd never gotten involved in your mad schemes."

"But you are."

"God forgive me," he continued in that same low, urgent voice. "How you ever persuaded me is beyond my comprehension, but you caught me at a weak moment. Or maybe you have magic powers and put a curse on me, or you're a first class negotiator."

"All of the above. But once this matter is over, you'll never have to lay eyes on me again."

"Thank heaven for that."

The fact of coming separation hung in the air between them, and she felt uncomfortable as she realized she would miss him. Sir Richard gave her a sense of solidity, someone who hadn't grown up with any strangeness around him. Sir Richard was so *normal,* she thought, something she craved.

"I daresay I should be grateful for not having to interact with your schemes again," he added with less vehemence.

"I'm hoping we can end this charade quickly," Jill said. "However, Laura won't part with her pendant at any cost."

"I don't blame her," he replied cynically. "I wouldn't either, if only on principle. You have no right to it, not really."

"Yes, I do!" she said heatedly and everyone glanced at her. She nodded and smiled as if to say that everything was in order.

"You *think* you do, but there's no guarantee that anything would change if you get the damned pendant." He cleared his throat. "I'm sorry for such impoliteness."

"For some reason, I'm not surprised at your choice of words."

Their eyes fought a battle of wills, but Jill felt a ridiculous urge to laugh. It bubbled in her throat and spilled over her lips. She saw his lips twitch in response.

"We are rather stubborn, wouldn't you think?" she commented.

He lifted his eyebrows in mock surprise. "Me? Balderdash."

"I prove my point," she said. "Do you have any suggestions that would further my cause quickly, like you stealing it from Laura's neck in her sleep?"

"You would suggest that I enter a maiden's bedchamber at night and steal her jewelry? Never."

"I spoke in jest. Heaven forfend that you would try anything adventurous."

"It would be highly inappropriate."

"Who would find out? Laura's doddering abigail? I'm sure she sleeps soundly through the night, starting at six in the evening. Laura doesn't have the heart to replace her."

"Yes, I see. I wouldn't have to bludgeon her in the dark to get to the pendant."

"You don't have to sound so sarcastic about it," she admonished.

He sighed. "I highly dislike the idea of parting Laura from her heirloom. It must mean a lot to her if she wears it all the time."

"I'm not without heart, and ever since I arrived at the Keep, I've been eaten with guilt, but I have my mission, which is more serious than her grief at losing an old rock."

"I only know what you've told me and your father's account of the past, but none of that has proved that this is not something a fevered mind concocted."

"I understand your reluctance, but the past is true. My family has suffered enough, and I have the understanding to end it all."

"With your determination you should've been part of the Crusades. You would have accomplished a great deal."

"Mayhap, but this mission is much smaller obviously." She gave him a calculating stare. "You're the only one who can achieve the desired result. You'll have to find a way to claim the pendant. She is not resistant to you."

"When it comes to such intimate details, I'm sure she is, Miss Ashcroft."

She clapped a hand to her mouth. "Don't call me that!" she ordered under her breath. "You could ruin everything if Laura heard that name."

"You do understand that I consider you a lunatic," he commented.

"It matters not," she replied haughtily. "So, what is your suggestion? You have yet to give me any plan of action."

"Because I don't have one. I don't consider it my responsibility to abscond with Laura's heirloom. You are entirely on your own."

She pouted, annoyed with his inflexibility. "If you want to see the back of me, you may have to help, you know."

"I don't want to repeat myself."

"Very well, I shall find a solution, but don't scowl at me every time you see me, as it may take some time."

"I have no doubt I'll hear an outcry before long, and I'll make sure I'll be at Laura's side to comfort her when the theft has been discovered."

"Theft is a rather crude word in this case."

"But one that is appropriate."

Jill fought an urge to curse him long and loud. He was right of course, and that's what made her angry. If only there could be another way, but as far as she knew, only one Endicott pendant existed, the one that Lucinda had imbued with her evil spells—may she rot in hell. "Perhaps I can find a way to replace the pendant, and she'll never be the wiser."

"That is the first sound suggestion I've heard from you, and I propose that you do just that. I don't want my fiancée to suffer any kind of heartache."

What would it be like to have someone care about you intimately? Jill wondered. She had taken care of herself—and her father—most of her life.

Brumley, the butler, bowed and opened the doors to the dining room. Candles sparkled in two massive silver candelabra on the table, throwing pools of golden light in the room where the ceiling soared into pitch darkness, and the walls loomed thick and uninviting around them. The table had been set beautifully with a white damask tablecloth and glittering crystal. Fruit of all colors and shapes spilled over from a porcelain basket in the center, and after Jill had been seated, she leaned over and nipped a branch of red grapes from a cluster, and started eating.

Julian sat to her right, Edgar to her left, and she glanced at Laura at the head of the table with Sir Richard on her right. He would soon be sitting at the head, she thought, and it made her uncomfortable.

His presence always had the power to make her world tilt, and she didn't know how to deal with the feelings he triggered. One moment she was angry, the next ready to laugh, or scream at something frustrating that he'd uttered. The control she had over her world seemed to be slipping away.

"Laura is a gracious hostess," Jill said, just to open the conversation with her companions. She'd noticed Julian's narrowed glance as Laura had responded to Sir Richard's gallant toast to her.

"She reminds me of the puppies I have, always so full of trust, seeing only the best in everyone around them," Julian said. "She never lost that trait." He paused. "I will see to it that Sir Richard treats her with utmost respect, or he'll have to answer to me," he said with a cold edge.

"Sir Richard is *made of* solid respect, you must see as much," Jill said, and sent a disdainful glance at Julian. "It would surprise me if you cannot."

"Hmm, he seems rather dictatorial," Julian mused, and Jill fought an urge to send a sharp elbow into his side.

"Dictatorial? Fustian. He may have firm opinions but that doesn't make him domineering. For what I know of him, he's a fair man." And that was true, she realized.

"I would be delighted to hold her close in a waltz," Edgar said in his nasally voice, and Jill shivered.

Jill didn't like his suggestive comment. "I'd be surprised if she would know how to dance the waltz." She gave his shirt points a contemptuous stare. "Besides, you would probably stab her in the eyes with those before she even took the first step."

"Of all the brazen—" Edgar began, puffing himself up.

"Ah! A termagant," Julian said, coolly pleasant. "I don't hear anyone criticize your gown or choice of gloves, Miss Iddings."

"That's neither here nor there. I would certainly not want to waltz with anyone whose face is mostly concealed behind starched linen."

Jill regretted those words, as they stirred up animosity, but the young man looked ridiculous with his puce waistcoat, sandy curls plastered to his forehead with pomade, and shoulder pads so wide they dwarfed the rest of his body. Julian at least had the common sense to dress simply and elegantly in a black coat and well-fitting knee breeches.

"Your outspoken demeanor is charming to a degree," Julian began with one of his best smiles. "But can appear unnerving to someone of a less robust character." He leaned closer and touched her hand. "I don't mind fire in a female. It makes for lively interaction."

She wasn't sure if his suave words held innuendo, but she suspected as much. There was no doubt he could charm her, but she wasn't going to let him. He had an edge that somehow spelled out danger, a worldliness of a kind that she had never experienced. Only for that reason she didn't quite trust him.

they're letting themselves down on those strands that they make, right onto your bed, or somewhere else where you don't want them. Life can be very trying sometimes, or as my friend Alf says, 'life has many pitfalls.' There's danger at every turn."

Jill thought his reasoning flawed. "I daresay not that many people expire from inhaling mosquitoes, and rarely do you hear of people dying from stepping on an ant. Spiders usually live in dark corners waiting for prey."

Edgar shivered again. "I can see the gruesome picture in my mind's eye, and it makes me sick." He pushed aside his fish dish. "There's no telling what really went into this meal, you know."

"Really, Edgar," Julian said, "I think you're boring Miss Iddings with your phobias. I doubt she would ever be able to understand your terror. She doesn't seem to be the type that suffers from irrational fears, or fear of any kind."

"Thank you, Lord Sandhurst. I am blessed to be quite unafraid. And I daresay this course holds only fish as this is a respectable establishment."

Edgar's nostrils quivered, and she sensed he was about to say something strong, but relented. He threw cautious glances at Sir Richard and Laura in turn.

"We are all guests here, and the least we can do is to treat our gracious hosts with respect," she whispered to this spoiled young man whom she wished she'd never met. "And Laura's chef is first class." She turned a cold shoulder and addressed the viscount.

"According to Laura, you're quite an adventurer. Have you done a lot of traveling?"

He nodded, his gaze roving around the room instead of staying with her. He embodied restlessness, and she suspected he had too much time on his hands.

"I've seen many parts of the world. When I was younger I sailed to the West Indies, the Americas, and to many of the countries on the Continent. That was part of my education. Spent some time in Italy painting in the style of the great masters."

"You're a man of talent then," she said.

"I followed in my cousin's footsteps, until he passed away. But that's many years ago now."

"You live alone at Sandhurst, then?" Jill wanted to know more about this man but she sensed he was reluctant to speak about himself.

"Oh no, my grandmother, Lady Georgina, lives there. She's rather long in the tooth, and quite doddery, which is a real pity. More often than not, she can't remember her own name." He indicated Edgar with his head. "This whippersnapper appears in the area on and off, but he likes the metropolis better."

"Yes . . . I can see that." Jill sighed, wondering if she'd ever see London again, or if the curse would get to her before she had a chance to dispel it. She never knew when it would strike, but it seemed that several of her relatives had demised around a full moon.

"London has its allure," Julian said when she lost the thread of the conversation.

"For a man of the world, do you find our capital more colorless and dull than, say, Paris?"

"Not at all!" he said with vehemence. "The exotic places I visited had lots to offer—better weather for one—but I prefer the sophistication and the elegance of London."

"Theaters and gaming salons," she added, perhaps to goad him, but he didn't react in a negative manner.

Treat yourself to 4 FREE Regency Romances!
A $19.96 VALUE... FREE!
No obligation to buy anything ever!

REGENCY ROMANCE BOOK CLUB
Zebra Home Subscription Service, Inc.
P.O. Box 5214
Clifton NJ 07015-5214

"The very best." He drank more wine as the lackeys served all the guests.

A platter of beef was carried in. Another footman bore a tray with bowls of peas and roasted potatoes. Jill felt slightly tipsy from drinking too much wine, but it also made her relax. Everything took on a lighter glow and for a moment she could forget her mission and just enjoy the company of the people at the table—well, for the most part.

Julian said, loud enough for everyone to hear. "I met that strange gypsy woman when I went out riding this morning."

"The one who lives by herself in the woods on the far side of the village?" Laura asked. "At the edge of the moor."

Julian nodded. "She was muttering to herself in Romany and shook her fist at me as I passed. That wild white hair straggled around her face, and she looked as gnarled as one of the tree trunks beside which she stood."

" 'Tis said she's quite mad. I've never met her, but I've heard tales that she claims kinship with the Endicotts. She's very old, perhaps ninety, if not older."

"I've never heard of her," Jill said, wondering if the lady would know anything about the Ashcroft curse.

"How could you?" Laura asked. "This is the first time you visit here."

Jill couldn't very well tell them she'd investigated in depth the past of the Endicott family. "You're right, of course. I'm just making conversation."

Sir Richard gave her an incredibly stern look, and she cringed inwardly. "What's her name, or don't you know?" she forged on.

"Tula. No one knows where she comes from, but

she's been here for most of her life as far as I know,"
Laura said.

"She lives in the woods?" Jill prodded.

Laura nodded. "She has a little cottage and some
fields she used to work. I doubt she does anymore, but
some of the local farmers keep her in victuals. It is
said she cultivates beautiful flowers around her house,
but I don't know as I've never seen for myself."

Mayhap you will, Jill thought. *I plan to.*

Nine

True to her word, Jill rode out the next afternoon with the aim of locating Tula, the gypsy woman. She got lost on the vast moor, and for a while she feared she would have to spend the night in cold isolation among the heather. The shadows were lengthening, darkness creeping in, as she heard hoofbeats coming toward her on one of the paths she'd investigated earlier.

She would never be able to find her way in the dark. Sir Richard appeared, looking incredibly annoyed.

"Blast and damn," he swore as he reined in at her side. "I knew I would find you here, and don't give me any lies about getting lost. You went in search of that mad gypsy woman, didn't you?"

She nodded. "Yes. . . . I thought she might be able to shed some light on the Endicott pendant and its history." She glanced around, finding they were alone. "The others?"

"Laura is searching the cliff path, and she sent Julian off in the opposite direction. She's worried you've taken a fall and broken a bone. But I knew better." The last words came out with vitriol.

"You have no right to berate me," she cried.

"Yes, I do, when I have go out in search of you. It'll be pitch black before we can get back, and I'm not sure about the direction of all of these paths. Straight West ought to be the sea."

"If you're trying to make me feel guilty, you're failing miserably," she said. "I have the right to ride and explore without receiving lectures from you."

"Not without a groom! What in the world made you do something so foolhardy? It's easy to get lost on the moor. You don't know the area, nor do you know the inhabitants. Not everyone is friendly around here."

"You for one," she cried.

He halted his horse, wheeled around and sidled up to her mount so close her leg squeezed between the animals' bodies. "What are you doing?"

He took the reins from her hand and pulled the horse to a halt. Leaning so close she could smell the scent of his soap and that alluring masculinity, he shouted at her. "I've had enough of your saucy tongue, Miss Ashcroft. Every time I look at you, my anger boils to the surface."

"I have done nothing to make you angry—not intentionally," Jill said, her blood starting to heat up. The gall of the man! She tried to pull the reins back, and the horses were mauling her leg, until she rubbed up against Sir Richard's leg.

"Rubbish. You have done nothing but," he growled. "How can you be here, eating Laura's food, drinking her wine, talking to her friends without a care in the world. Have you no conscience?"

"Of course I do," she shouted at him. "Do you think I enjoy bamboozling her, the most innocent and kind person I've ever known?" Jill tossed her head. "Anyway, I can only be myself, and I don't cower in some corner. And Laura, she deserves better than you," she added to goad him more. The man always managed to make her angry.

"She deserves better than us . . . both," he spat. "I

don't enjoy subterfuge of any kind, but you seem to thrive on it."

"That's a bold untruth. As a rule, I'm straightforward and open." She still tried to tear the reins from him, and the horses were getting agitated.

Suddenly, he bent forward and gripped one lapel of her riding jacket. He looked diabolical in the last orange rays of the sun, and his eyes flashed dark fire. She thought he would try to strangle her.

So this might be her moment, her violent death by strangling, she thought, dazed, but all at once perfectly lucid as if she could see every minute detail of her life with absolute clarity. He pulled her close, and she would have fallen to the ground if he hadn't held her so tightly.

Before she had a chance to defend herself, his mouth came down on hers. Her head started spinning as a current of something exploded in her veins. She was only aware of his mouth, the soft texture, the demanding pressure, and the sweetness that made her weak inside. Just as suddenly as he'd gripped her, he let go of her.

She clung to the horn of her sidesaddle and straightened her precarious position. He stared at her for a long moment, as if unable to believe what had just transpired.

She touched her lips, then her jacket, and realized her hat sat askew on her head. Her mare danced away, and Jill didn't say a word to Sir Richard, who seemed to have lost his voice as well.

She gained control of her horse and readjusted her hat and her jacket. Sir Richard was riding behind her on the path, a silent menace that spelled nothing but unrest. She'd never counted on this to happen.

When she could find her unsteady voice, she asked,

"Why did you do that, Sir Richard? Is there something written in our agreement that you can take advantage of me?"

"I . . . no, I don't know what came over me. Frustration, I suppose." He took a deep breath. "I'm sorry."

"You wanted to hit me."

"Of course not! I've never hit a female."

She knew he spoke the truth. She suspected it had been wildly out of character for him to kiss her with such animal passion. He was, or he liked to think he was, the epitome of male gallantry. Somehow she inspired his baser nature.

"I won't tell a soul what happened, and I'm sure you won't either," she said. "Just a moment of temporary madness."

He barked a laugh. "You're right—madness."

They rode on in silence, encountering no one. Before long she spied the long, winding drive that led to the Keep. "You knew very well where we were," she said to him, "but you wanted me to suffer the agony of guilt."

"I had to interrupt my afternoon with Laura to search for you. Everyone has been worried about you, especially your aunt, so I suggest you ride straight to her."

Chastened, Jill did just that, and Aunt Iddy embraced her with a cry of relief. "I thought you might've fallen off the cliffs into the sea."

Aunt Iddy knew how possible that could be under the current circumstances of the curse hanging over them, but Jill didn't mention it, only hugged her aunt tight. "I'm fine. I got somewhat lost on the moor. 'Tis easy to lose direction out there." She gestured to Sir Richard standing behind her. "He has a good sense of direction."

Aunt Iddy thanked him profusely, and Laura stepped into the foyer, Julian right beside her. She looked relieved as well, a big smile wreathing her face. "I knew we would find you hale and hearty."

Jill embraced her. "Thank you." Now the guilt did come along, a big suffocating wave.

Julian eyed her narrowly, and she wondered if he could sense her duplicity. She shrugged it off, not paying him any attention.

"The moor can be very treacherous, especially at night, or in the fog. If you ride far enough into it, everything looks exactly the same," Laura said.

"I realize that now," Jill replied. "I won't do it again, not without a groom following me."

She still had a desire to see Tula, but perhaps she could get someone who knew where the old woman lived to come with her.

Julian was still staring at her thoughtfully, but she wouldn't ask him. For some reason she wouldn't feel safe with him, not as she did with Sir Richard even if he had compromised her. She found it difficult to explain that logic to herself. It made no sense at all.

Everyone was staring at her, she noticed. Could they see the imprint of his kiss on her mouth, or had the word "traitor" been emblazoned on her forehead? She touched her hat, finding that it sat straight. "Is something wrong?" she asked.

"We're just grateful that you're here now," Aunt Iddy said, breaking the silence.

Jill thanked them all again. Not daring to look at Sir Richard's menacing eyes, she took herself upstairs to her room. She sank down on her bed, putting her tired head on the pillows. Instead of dwelling on the curse as she usually did, she kept seeing Sir Richard's face coming closer and closer to her own, and then the wild pressure of his mouth on hers.

How could she ever really face Laura again? How could he? But she hadn't started the madness, he had.

Madness it was, but how wonderful it had felt. Never before had anyone kissed her in a way that touched her all the way down to her toes. Mostly she'd been the recipient of brotherly pecks and fatherly hugs.

Her imagination always was fertile, but it would never have been able to cook up such a wonderful sensation as Sir Richard's kiss had given her.

Sir Richard felt the harsh fire of guilt keenly every time he looked into Laura's kind eyes. He couldn't believe what had come over him, this mad desire to kiss some sense into Jillian Ashcroft. Not that he could believe that excuse wholeheartedly; he'd kissed her because he'd desired to, as simple as that.

Her damned seductive mouth had tasted of honey and excitement, which had taken him with much surprise. The woman wasn't exactly sweet, far from it.

Or had he judged her completely wrongly? God, he hoped not, because if he had, he feared the memory of the kiss would nag him forever.

Jill got her wish to see Tula the very next day although she hadn't planned on it. She rode down to Pendenny village with Laura to buy a spool of thread, and when they returned, Laura suggested they go by way of the woods.

Mostly the moor stretched in every direction, but in a pocket between the village and the sea grew a small forest. Perhaps it had been planted in the distant past, but the trees certainly wouldn't tell the story of how they'd come about.

"I like the solitude among the oaks," Laura said. "The sunlight never looks mysterious and green like this around the Keep."

"The trees filter it beautifully."

Laura looked at her questioningly. "Richard never told me where you're from, Jill. Is your home near Eversley?"

Jill decided she couldn't lie. "No . . . my family hails from Devon originally."

"Oh." Laura frowned as if deep in thought. "I know of a family from Devon—enemies of ours. A long, long time ago, much before my time. I have no reason to keep up some old feud, but my father spoke of some ancient ill done to the Endicotts. It's all in some accounts in the library. Do you know—?"

"Look over there," Jill distracted her and pointed at a convenient woodpecker drumming at a tree trunk.

Laura followed her direction and they both saw the old woman standing in a small clearing near the busy bird. She looked wild, her white hair a tangle around her face, and her shawl and skirt mended so many times it was impossible to see the original fabric.

"It's Tula," Laura whispered.

Tula moved forward, her thin hand wrapped around a tall stick that had been carved and adorned with feathers and seedpods.

Jill's heart started pounding. This woman looked formidable, someone who could harm you should she take a dislike to you. "Good morning," Jill greeted cautiously.

The old woman's black gaze bored into her, and she felt as if all of her secrets had been ripped open. Then Tula looked at Laura, her gaze even more intense.

"You step into my forest unbidden?" she growled.

Laura pulled a purse from her pocket and poured a handful of coins into Tula's hand. "We're only using the woods as a shortcut to the Keep."

"You're her then? The young one, the last Endicott?"

Laura nodded. "And this is my friend Jill Iddings."

Jill swallowed hard, fearing the woman would reveal all in one sentence, but she only stared at Jill for a long moment. She turned anew to Laura. "I heard you're planning a wedding."

"Yes . . . a few weeks hence. Not a large affair, but—"

"A large affair you deserve, young woman. Why settle for something paltry?" Tula asked gutturally. "He doesn't treat you with the respect you deserve."

"Sir Richard?" Laura sounded incredulous. "He's wholly respectful, and gentlemanly in every way."

"But cold," Tula warned. "Caution to you." She looked at Jill, who felt herself blushing. It must be true that Tula had the ability to "see."

Tula pointed at Jill. "You're made of fire where this young lady is made of air." She made a sweeping motion with her arm in Jill's direction. "There's a black cloud surrounding you."

"Really?" Jill asked, fear gripping her. "Do you actually see it?"

Tula nodded, her pointy chin quivering. "It has been with you for a long time . . . longer than you know."

"That is strange," Laura protested. "Jill is the most positive and energetic woman I know."

"Aye, she has a bright fire, but something is fighting her, and those she loves."

Jill needed no more confirmation. She had no doubt Tula could see the very curse. But she didn't want the old woman to start talking about curses and bring memories back to Laura, who clearly had forgotten all that her father had told her.

Tula continued, "Beware of a devious young man with blue eyes."

Laura and Jill glanced at each other. They knew several gentlemen with blue eyes, but Jill immediately thought of Alvin Ashcroft, whom she knew would make things difficult for her if he could.

"He will trick you."

"Which one of us?" Laura asked.

Tula fell silent for a while. "There are *two* men with blue eyes."

"How odd," Jill said *sotto voce*.

Tula continued. "Lots of tears, thunder, and lightning before this is over, but it shall pass." She looked straight at Jill, who felt a stab of guilt. "You have to hold the course strong or you shall be next—with the man with blue eyes. There's a fork in the road and you must choose wisely."

A wave of icy fear coursed through Jill, then a sudden heat, and she knew the woman had spoken the truth.

"I don't know what you're talking about, Tula," Laura said pleasantly, "but I promise to be careful."

Jill mumbled a thank you and wheeled her mare around on the narrow path. She needed to leave with haste.

"That was strange," Laura said behind her as they'd left the woods. "Tula spoke in riddles. Could you make any sense of it?"

Jill shook her head. "I'm confused. She's full of blarney, don't you think?"

Laura rode up beside her on the moor as the horses ambled along. She shrugged. "I don't know, but she has a good reputation for *knowing*."

"Yes . . . perhaps, but she can't always be right."

"Perhaps not. It was peculiar how she mentioned I deserve a large wedding."

"Well, don't you? It would befit your station. I'm surprised Sir Richard doesn't insist on it."

"He's not one for extravagance, and he probably worries about the expense even if I have plenty of funds. I really don't care much." She sighed forlornly. "I know it should be the most glorious day of my life . . ."

"But—?" Jill prompted as her friend's voice petered out.

"I have no idea what to expect," Laura said. "Sir Richard courts me in a most proper manner, but I wish he would show a bit more . . . you know. . . ." She blushed, and Jill knew.

Appalled, she thought of the fire that Sir Richard had shown *her*, not his bride to be. It was the outside of enough, and so she would tell him next time she came across him. He'd been avoiding her since that kiss yesterday. It was about time he started showing his passion for Laura.

"Perhaps he's afraid of overstepping his bounds," she said feebly.

"I doubt that Richard suffers from a great deal of fear, and he's well-versed in interaction with females."

Laura was right in that respect. Sir Richard did not lack in confidence, and Jill doubted he would have difficulty showing his bride some of the romance to come.

Laura's lips drooped at the corners. "I didn't like the encounter with Tula. I wonder what she meant by a dark cloud hanging around you."

"Mayhap she saw a cloud of frustration or fatigue. I have been tired lately," Jill fibbed.

"Yes . . . after a whirlwind Season in London, I daresay you would be tired."

They rode on in silence for a moment. Laura shielded her eyes against the glare of the sun. "I'm surprised you aren't engaged or promised to someone. If I were a gentleman, I think I would find you intriguing."

Jill laughed. "Thank you. I suspect the gentlemen shy away from females with minds of their own."

"Are you suggesting they like vapid and mindless females?"

Jill thought about that momentarily. "It wouldn't be far off the mark."

"A lowly opinion indeed," Laura said, her expression aghast. "You're too young to be so cynical."

Jill laughed. "If you met all the nincompoops I encountered in London, you would be of the same opinion. Imagine hundreds of Edgars around you."

Laura clapped her hand to her mouth. "Gentlemen like Edgar? *That* would sorely try my patience."

"So you're not a saint or an angel after all."

Laura laughed. "Jill, you're so entertaining. My life was unbearably dull before you came here."

"I doubt that very much. You have your beloved animals. They must curse the day I set foot here to take your attention away from them."

Laura's laughter spilled out anew. "That is possibly true, but I haven't noticed any vindictiveness among them."

"God bless their little souls," Jill said with mock piety. She thought of the four-footed parade that often followed Laura, and the unbidden image of spiteful horses stomping on her foot and malicious cats urinating on her shoes made her giggle.

"Why are you laughing?"

"I thought of things your animals might do to give me my comeuppance."

"I doubt they would do anything but look upon you with joy and trust."

"I can tell you don't know horses and cats very well," Jill said with a grimace. "I've had my fair share of encounters with annoyed animals."

"They are easier to get along with than gentlemen, don't you think?" Laura said wistfully.

"That I do believe. Do I detect some hesitation in your voice?"

"I feel so inexperienced. I don't know what Sir Richard expects of me, and he hasn't spoken of it. I have no idea if I please him, or if I annoy him."

"Don't worry about it. If he were displeased, you would know about it, believe me. He's a gentleman who doesn't mind speaking up for himself."

They neared the Keep and the dogs came charging and barking joyously across the old moat area and the park.

"I suppose I should put my fears to rest," Laura said with a sigh.

"Time will give you experience," Jill replied. "Everything will be fine," she added, wondering if that were true.

Ten

Jill went into the library that afternoon when everybody had retired for a rest before dinner. She wanted to look for the account of the Endicotts that Laura had mentioned earlier. Perhaps she could glean some fact she didn't already know.

To her surprise, she found Sir Richard ensconced in a wing chair with a glass of wine at his elbow and a book in his hand.

He lifted an eyebrow at her, and she suspected he thought she had followed him here, as if she didn't have anything better to do.

"Don't let me disturb you, Sir Richard," she said haughtily. "I'm looking for a particular book, and when I find it I'll leave. I promise to keep quiet."

"That must be a great challenge for you," he replied smoothly.

"No need to get into an argument over such a small thing," she said. "I didn't seek you out to cross swords."

Her heart racing with the unexpected encounter, she inspected the titles of the many leather bound books in the stacks. They smelled faintly of mold and dust. She abhorred the fact that his very presence could make her heartbeat escalate in any way.

"I'm not surprised to see you here as you seem to have a penchant for books."

She decided not to reply. Studying the gold

lettering on a particularly aged tome, she pretended not to hear him.

"I suppose reading is a lighter endeavor than deciphering old curses," he continued, his voice airy.

She still didn't deign to reply; she would not let him goad her into an angry retort.

"The lighter fare is in the case under the window," he added helpfully. "The latest endeavors by Jane Austen and Maria Edgeworth. Something that might fit the female taste splendidly."

She balled her hands into fists. If he uttered one more word, she would surely strike him, and she wouldn't hesitate to aim right at his nose. *He's a most unbearable man,* she thought. Why did she ever have to involve him in her schemes?

"I can tell you're raring to fight with me, but I've no desire," she said as calmly as she could. She closed her eyes and pulled in her breath very slowly. "All I'm here to do is to find a book, and you're here, reading. That's all."

"But I have to look at you every day at the table," he said.

"How inconvenient for you," she said icily. "If you don't want to any longer, just find a way to get the Endicott pendant, and I shall be out of your life for good. Some quick action might bring you the desired results."

He glared at her as if saying "leave me out of this," but he must have remembered that he invited her to the Keep in the first place. "'Tis quite clear that your ancestors had more hair than wit; just look at your reason for being here."

"Then you must be just as addlebrained to play the 'game' with me," she returned, just as she found a stack of papers wrapped in leather, all held together with a sturdy thong.

"I expect it to be over shortly—it has to be. I'd have thought you'd be gone by now, your mission accomplished."

She didn't deign to answer that. "Sir Richard, you must've digested something with breakfast that didn't agree with you. It's clear to see you're very bilious."

He laughed coolly and shook his head. Taking a sip from his wine, he studied her face. She longed to just ignore him and march out of the room, but for some strange reason, he held her attention. She could not explain where this fascination for him stemmed from, and it bothered her terribly.

He indicated her bundle with his hand. "What are you going to read?"

"The history of Endicott, or some of it. To go back as far as the thirteenth century would take a long time."

"Which you don't have."

"As you keep reminding me. Perhaps there's something written in this account about the Ashcroft curse. It covers the time of Lucinda the Evil, but it was written in the last century, so there's no telling how much will be lost in the mists of time."

"Most of it surely, except for the glorious deeds of Endicott ancestors."

"I daresay you're right, but I always look at everything to get a greater picture."

"Why don't you speak of the curse to Laura?" he suggested.

"She's told me several times that she would never part with the pendant, so why risk her wrath? She's compassionate enough, but would probably take my deception poorly. I must have the pendant, or face the end of my family, and probably myself."

"You cannot be sure of that," he said. "I don't care

how many demises and accounts of strange deaths
you had in your family. It could just be coincidence."

"If it were, I wouldn't feel prompted to act upon my
inner conviction."

He lips curled at the corners. "Or maybe as I main-
tain, you have a bee in your bonnet—as do all of the
Ashcrofts."

"If you keep affirming this, I shall place a curse on
your family," she threatened, unable to find another
counter offer. "I shall turn you all into toads."

"I'm quivering in my boots," he said, and she
longed to fling the bundled writings in her hands at
him. She closed her eyes for a moment and took a
deep breath.

"You're not going to get my goat, Sir Richard. I
won't stoop to your level, nor will I stand here and
listen further. If you think I'm overset with grati-
tude or deference at your observations, you're sadly
mistaken."

She gave him a withering stare. Without another
word, she marched out of the room. She knew he was
laughing behind her back, plague take him!

She boiled with anger every time she thought about
him, but she pushed him resolutely aside as she fo-
cused on the written pages in front of her on the
escritoire in her bedchamber. The writer, a George
Fredrick Endicott, had penned the pages with a long
loping style, anno 1750. The scholar of that generation of the family, she thought.

She found his writing rather interesting as he went
into the family's exploits with the East India Company, and their trade with vessels named as exotically
as *Star of India,* and *Oriental Pearl.* It was clear the ships
had brought good fortune to the family, which Laura
still enjoyed today. It was rather obvious by the size of

the staff and the state of the Keep that Laura suffered no economic hardships, and never would.

The account also described a large pendant made from a ruby that a raja had given one the Endicotts in India. *I will have to ask Laura about that,* she thought. Rubies were considered gems of power and potency, and of great luxury. It would be interesting to see it.

George Fredrick mentioned the Endicott pendant once, as a good luck charm that had brought wealth and safety to the family. He claimed it came from the ancient Celtic or Norse people, something that may have been found in the earth and made sacred, but who could know for sure if it were that old? She couldn't find any mention of Lucinda, but didn't really expect any. No family would boast of the fact that one of their members had been a witch. That is if they really *knew* the truth about Lucinda.

"You're really digging into things that will lead nowhere," she said to herself.

Sighing, she kept on reading just in case she would find something that would explain the past. What she could use was a family tree, but she hadn't come across one. Her father had made one, unearthed the old connections through the Ashcroft history, but there were gaps and she assumed the Endicotts' tree looked similar.

"All I need is the pendant," she said out loud.

She jumped with fright as a knock sounded on the door.

Laura stepped inside without prompting. She looked rather excited, Jill thought.

"We've been invited to a gathering at Lady Pen-holly's in Tregary. She and I are distant relatives, but I rarely see her because she spends most of her time in London. She is an interesting lady—rather unconventional, as she has traveled widely to all sorts of exotic locales. Never married, never wished to. She claims it would curb her freedom."

"Another bluestocking, Sir Richard would say," Jill said with a wry smile.

"I daresay you're right." Laura leaned over the escritoire. "It's flattering to me that you would interest yourself in the history of Endicott Keep. It has been rather a blood-soaked place I'm afraid, full of pride and battle."

Jill nodded. "Yes, it's described in detail." Silently she added that she wasn't really interested in that.

"I'm grateful the violence is no longer part of our history."

Jill decided to probe a little. "I read about a famous ruby here. Do you have it still?"

Laura shook her head. "It went to another branch of the family when Father died. I saw it once." She sighed with longing. "It was spectacular."

"I've heard it said your family had knowledge of . . . of the magical arts."

Laura thought for a moment, biting her lip as if debating how to approach the subject. "Some say, but I have no real proof that we had facts that came down through the ages. It would've been ancient knowledge about the nature of energy, that which can't be seen with these eyes."

Jill nodded, her heart hammering, and her hands beginning to tremble.

"Our lineage has French, Hungarian, and Russian blood, and the ancient arts must've been carried forward through that heritage. My great-grandfather is said to have had the ability to look into the future, and I have to admit that I sometimes sense things.

Perhaps you can call it premonition. I don't always relish the feelings I get."

"I understand," Jill replied, barely finding her voice. "I also receive impressions of things to come. I suppose that's why I have somewhat of an interest in these things."

"Yes, but I doubt anything is written down about that in the accounts. The knowledge was handed down verbally, and no one of my parents' generation ever spoke of it. My grandfather told me to trust my feelings because therein lies the truth, but he never mentioned anything about magic."

Jill looked at the Endicott pendant around Laura's neck, and she longed to bring that up, but how could she? The deception had gone too far for the truth to be revealed now.

As if Laura felt Jill's attention, she fingered the stone for a long moment, her expression troubled. "I don't know, but I sense agitation. Perhaps all I feel is nerves for the upcoming nuptials."

Jill knew it wasn't the whole truth, but how could she say anything without implicating herself and her deception?

"You'll see that everything will end well," she said without conviction. Guilt nagged at her ever more strongly. "You're nervous about change, that's all."

Sir Richard couldn't find a satisfying explanation why his mind kept revolving around Jillian Ashcroft. The woman was nothing but a thorn in his side, and he knew the only way to get rid of her for good was to get the blasted pendant. He had to get rid of her if he were ever to get closer to Laura. He glanced at the ladies sitting at the table.

Since breakfast, Laura and the Misses Endicott and Iddings had been poring over the fashion plates sent down from London, and there was no sign of Jillian. Evidently she had no interest in the latest fashions, or she was avoiding him. Both, he thought. He hadn't seen her since yesterday afternoon in the library.

Laura looked rosy and quite excited about the dresses she would order from London for her trousseau, and he wished he could feel something other than brotherly concern for her. Maybe if he made some real effort, he might break through to some deeper feelings. He put down the news sheet he'd been reading and rose.

"Come, my dear, let's take a stroll in the garden. The morning is exceptionally beautiful—just as you are."

She looked up at him and smiled. Putting down the picture of an evening gown, she stood. "Yes . . . if you want to, I'd be delighted." She retrieved the white fringed shawl she'd dropped on one of the chairs and draped it over her shoulders. Her maid brought a straw hat to protect Laura's complexion against the sun, and out they went.

The sun was shining with the bright clear light of spring. The breeze played gently around them, and birds sang in every tree. The sea glittered and rolled in the sunlight, and daffodils and hyacinths nodded in borders along the walls. He led her onto the path that wove through the vegetable garden and onto a stretch that had a magnificent view of the water. Wooden benches had been set down for the Keep's inhabitants to enjoy when the weather permitted.

They walked to the very end where a lookout point had been fenced in. Beyond it lay a steep gorge that separated this part of the shore from the rest of the mainland, a natural division that had protected the Keep from marauders in the past.

"Are you looking forward to the wedding?" Sir Richard asked and looked at Laura from the corner of his eye. She didn't look wildly enthusiastic, he thought.

"Ah, yes, of course," she said, sounding somewhat breathless.

Perhaps she was afraid of him. "I sense some hesitation in that reply," he prodded. "Do you fear my proximity?" He took her elbow and steered her to the bench by a gnarled, wind-whipped juniper.

She shook her head. "Not at all. I just don't know what to expect, or what is expected of me. I have lived a very simple life up till now."

He smiled, feeling tenderness for her honesty and animated face. "I don't expect anything of you, Laura. Just be yourself, and we shall get on splendidly."

He leaned over her, and she blushed fiercely. The pendant sat there at her throat, mocking him and reminding him of the subterfuge that he so abhorred. He took her face between his hands and tilted it back a little so that he could kiss her. As he moved his mouth to hers, he put one of his arms around her shoulder, gripping her neck gently.

She trembled in his arms, and he noticed she was holding her breath. Her eyelids fluttered as if in the throes of a nightmare. He sighed, and touched her lips with his own.

Concentrating on the clasp of the pendant at the back of her neck, he gently maneuvered it between his fingers. It had some kind of loop around a silver ball, and he quickly tried to undo it as he deepened the kiss. His heartbeat escalated from the effort—not from the kiss, something of which he was acutely aware. It worried him more than the risk of being found out stealing the pendant as he fiddled with the clasp.

Suddenly, she tore away, her breathing harsh against his face. She pushed at his chest and he had to let go of her, and the necklace. As he leaned back, she got up from the bench and went to stare out over the ocean. She seemed to be in a daze, and unaware of his recent fiddling with the Endicott pendant.

If only it would just fall off, he wished, noting that he had undone the clasp halfway.

"Is there something the matter?" he asked, knowing full well something bothered her immensely.

"I . . . I don't know. . . . I'm not used to kissing gentlemen." She put her hands to her burning cheeks.

"Do I frighten you?" he asked gently.

She nodded. "Yes . . . no, but I'm not sure. You're very forceful."

In his opinion, he'd been tender and considerate and wondered if she was inclined to overreact. "I'm sorry. I had no intention of pushing myself on you in any way. I only hoped to explore with you our more affectionate feelings."

She nodded, fiddling with her pendant and securing the fastening. *Damn, he thought.*

"Yes, Richard, I understand. Your intentions are noble and honest." She took a deep, trembling breath. "I'm the one at fault."

He shook his head, feeling like a cad. "No, not at all. You're everything that is sweet and kind." How to best deal with this? he wondered. He was betrothed to this woman, yet so far there seemed to be no warmer feelings on either side.

"We need to spend more time together," he said finally when she wouldn't speak. Her back turned

toward him looked defensive. "It's the only way to develop any kind of romantic feeling."

"Well, you *are* spending time here, so we're bound
to develop something . . . whatever it is," she said,
evading his gaze.

"As long as you're not afraid, we can always work on
the enthusiasm."

She turned toward him and smiled tentatively.
"Thank you for your patience, Richard."

"We have a whole lifetime. . . ." he said, his voice
fading. The thought of spending the rest of his life intimate with Laura seemed wrong somehow, and it
made him extremely uneasy.

"Yes . . . a very long time," she replied, a sigh heav-
ing visibly in her chest.

He ran across Jillian later that morning, but she
tried to avoid him. Their paths crossed in the upstairs
corridor where all the Endicott forefathers witnessed
their encounter from stiff picture frames.

"I have no desire to speak with you, Sir Richard,"
she said at her haughtiest. "I've seen no results in our
'mission' and I know I can't count on your support
any longer."

Her scorn galled him. "I did try, this morning, but
the clasp would not let go," he defended himself, but
regretted it immediately.

"Why even bother to mention it if it wasn't successful?" She turned her hot stare on him, and he knew
she was right. Why bring up defeat? "I just wanted to
let you know that I've tried."

"Not good enough. Use a knife or a pair of scissors
next time." She gave him her shoulder and stalked
off.

"And possibly cut one of Laura's jugulars?" he threw after her.

"If your aim is that poor, don't even try," she replied.

"It's not the aim that is the danger here."

She stopped and threw him a contemptuous stare over her shoulder. "Don't tell me you're fearful, Sir Richard."

"Fearful of what?"

"Your precious hide, mayhap?"

How damned ungrateful, he thought, vowing to ignore Jillian Ashcroft from now on. Who cared if the curse activated and she fell down dead on the spot?

Eleven

Jill couldn't believe her terrible misfortune when she ran into her cousin Alvin outside Lady Penholly's on the following Saturday evening. He had just climbed down from the carriage ahead of them and stared at her narrowly while Sir Richard helped her down from the coach, then assisted his fiancée.

"Well, well!" Alvin said to Jill as he walked toward her, rubbing his narrow chin. "Fancy you of all people being here tonight."

She pretended to slip, pushing Alvin out of earshot of the others. He stumbled back and gripped her arm.

"What are you doing here?" she whispered furiously. "And don't speak so loudly."

"I was invited to the gathering with my friend Edgar," he replied defensively. "What are *you* doing here? I thought you were still in Sussex."

"It's a long story, one which I don't have time to speak much about now."

"There'll be plenty of time later," he said with a leer. He peered over her shoulder. "Who is that beautiful blond young lady?"

"No one." She wanted to grip him and shake him. "Under no circumstances are you to divulge who I am in relation to you, do you understand? Your very future is at stake here. *Your very future!*" she repeated, hoping her scaring tactics would work, but knowing they rarely did.

"What would happen?" he asked suspiciously. He looked at her with those cold light blue eyes, and she wondered why she even wanted to save his skin.

Dispelling of the curse was for her future children, she reminded herself. All Alvin really wanted was her inheritance; it was all that mattered to him. She would have to play on that to make him cooperate.

"I'll pay your latest debts—up to a certain point—if you keep your mouth shut about our connection. Thank God there's no family resemblance."

"You're being cruel when all I want is to be sweet and court you," he whined and swept back the pale hair that had flopped over one eye. "You're the flower that I long to pluck," he added suggestively.

"Of all shabby suggestions. . . it shall *never* happen."

His lips turned downward at the corners. "I don't care about my debts . . . who says they have to be paid? But I do care about my future, *our* future. Because of Lindenwood we'll always be connected."

Jill knew she couldn't bludgeon Alvin into keeping his tongue. If he babbled, her mission would be in shambles. "Listen to me," she hissed, "I'm Jillian Iddings, and until a certain mystery is solved, your life is at stake."

That ought to quiet him, she thought desperately.

"My life?"

She nodded. "You're the next to succumb according to the Ashcroft curse," *or I am*, she added silently.

"Fustian. You're a complete thimblewit, Coz, but don't worry, I shall take care of you." He made as if to embrace her, and from the corner of her eye, she noticed Sir Richard watching them as he helped Laura retrieve her shoe, which had gotten stuck between two paving stones at the bottom of the stairs.

"Desist, you maw-worm," Jill hissed. She pushed

Alvin away and followed Sir Richard and Laura up to the front door to greet their hostess. All she could muster was a false smile.

"Who was that?" Laura asked, staring at Alvin.

"Someone who tried to enter my graces in London," Jill replied. At least that was true. Alvin never stopped, evidently thinking persistence would pay. "I turned down his advances, but he's still hoping that I will change my mind."

"He has nothing to recommend himself," Laura said. "My first impression is that I don't like him, and the way he tried to *maul* you."

Your impression is keen, Jill thought. But then it always would be because her ability flowed in her blood.

Their hostess looked strikingly beautiful in a gold gown with a matching turban. Her dark eyes flashed with pleasure, and she smiled widely. She held out both her hands to Laura.

"At last. It's been so long since I saw you, my dear," Maureen, Lady Penholly, cried. "You have lost none of your dew-soft qualities." She turned to Sir Richard. "And here he is, your fiancé, at last."

Sir Richard bent over her hand. "I've heard nothing but good things about you."

Lady Penholly laughed. "Oh, pooh. I don't want to hear that. I pride myself in going against the common current. You must know that I have a reputation for outrageous behavior. After all, I have all the liberal thinkers and artists at my salons, and our exploits always end up in the news sheets the next day."

"Sorry, but it slipped my mind," Sir Richard said with a smile.

Aren't you going to call her a bluestocking? Jill thought bitterly. She feigned a cough to give him her contempt via a raised eyebrow and a sardonic smile. He did send her a cursory glance that narrowed as he read her signal, but he looked away with an expression of disgust.

Maureen greeted Jill graciously. "Hmmm, you remind me of someone," she said, "oh yes, an astrologer I used to consult in my past. His name was Ash—"

"Oh no, I wouldn't be connected to someone with that kind of talent. My last name is Iddings, and we're quite a dull family." She saw Aunt Iddy open her mouth as if to protest, but Jill put a calming hand on her arm.

Aunt Iddy looked beautiful in a bronze-hued gown and a matching turban with ostrich feathers dyed black. Jet pearls hung around her neck.

Jill saw her cousin and Edgar walk up the steps to stand behind them. Thank God Laura and Sir Richard had moved ahead with Aunt Penny.

"Alvin, Edgar!" their hostess greeted them. "The younger contingent is gathering. I do so prefer young people around me, don't you agree?" she asked Aunt Iddy.

Aunt Iddy opened and closed her mouth. "Oh . . . ah, yes."

"They bring a lot of energy, don't they?"

"Well . . . yes," Aunt Iddy said, floundering.

Auntie would agree to anything, Jill thought, wondering if her aunt ever had an original thought. *Patience,* she told herself. Aunt Iddy had a heart of gold, a rather uncommon commodity, and she certainly never agreed with Jill.

Sir Richard on the other hand, had a heart made of stone. Laura deserved someone nicer. Just as she thought that, Julian, Viscount Sandhurst, joined them in the hallway.

"My dearest!" Lady Penholly cried, and Julian

kissed both of her cheeks, which spoke of much familiarity.

Aunt Iddy glanced from Alvin to Jill, her face a study of uneasiness. She opened her mouth as if to say something, but Jill squeezed her arm in warning.

"Maureen, I'm so delighted you decided to come home," Julian said. "The area has been dull without your musical laughter and inspired words." He turned to the others. "Maureen is an excellent poet."

"When the wine floweth, my tongue is loosened," the hostess said as one of the footmen carried through a tray of glasses filled with champagne. She urged everyone to take one, and as they moved into the brightly lit mansion full of colorful Oriental fabrics and flowers. Jill delighted in the view of comfort that greeted her.

Not a single suit of armor stood sentinel, and Jill felt as if she could breathe again. Lady Penholly had made the cavernous room with its marble columns and vast parquet floors welcoming. Guests milled about in the ballroom, which also sported musical instruments, among them a pianoforte. Jill suspected the hostess knew how to play rather well.

The room smelled sweetly of roses. Through the open doors, she could see climbing red blooms along the terrace, and winding around the pillars. She walked closer to the doors and noticed a profusion of flowers stretching as far as she could see into the garden.

"How lovely," she said to herself. "One day I shall have a peaceful haven just like this."

Laura approached her from one side, and Edgar and Alvin from the other. Panic ran through Jill's veins.

"Miss Laura, I want to present a dear friend of mine." He gestured to Alvin. "This is Mr. Alvin Ash—"

Jill fell into a fit of contrived coughing to interrupt the introduction. She waved her wine glass as if to explain that she'd swallowed wrong. Laura moved to slap her gently on the back, and she stood, leaning heavily on her friend's arm to distract her attention.

Alvin gave her a look of disgust, but Jill knew she'd averted a potential disaster. "I'm pleased to meet you, Miss Endicott, and I hope we'll get a chance to become better acquainted."

Laura smiled at him, but Jill noticed that it didn't reach her eyes. "Mr. Ash, surely you're much too busy to take any interest in my life," Laura said.

"'Pon rep, I should pray I'm not that shallow and self-serving," Alvin said.

That you are, Jill thought, and held her breath wondering if Edgar would correct Alvin's last name for Laura's benefit, but he was staring out the window at someone. He nudged Alvin in the side.

"By Jove, Edgar."

Edgar said, "Perhaps we should move on, Alvin, before we get a rake-down from the ladies' chaperones. There's someone I'd like you to meet."

They saw Aunt Iddy and Aunt Penny approaching, and Jill prayed Alvin wouldn't say something to Aunt Iddy that would ruin everything. He gave her an ill-tempered look, but only bowed stiffly. Arm in arm, the two young men sauntered off, their extremely high shirt points giving them the appearance of popinjays.

"Don't give us a rake-down for talking to the gentlemen," Laura pleaded to the aunts.

They shrugged their shoulders. "If there was any damage done, there would be nothing I could do to change it. I doubt, however, that your reputations can get ruined at this simple gathering in the country. There are no London gossip mongers here," Aunt Penny said.

"Except for the hostess herself," Aunt Iddy filled in, "but she's occupied elsewhere at this minute."

Sir Richard joined them and offered to fetch more drinks. Jill asked for some lemonade. Laura went to freshen up with the aunts as Sir Richard walked off.

Jill drew a sigh of relief that the impending disaster had been staved off—for now. To calm herself, she went outside and fanned her hot face.

"It is rather lovely," Sir Richard said a few minutes later, and she started. She hadn't heard him approach. He handed her the lemonade. "In fact, I take a keen interest in gardening, and Eversley is very much like this. The birds enjoy the grounds too as they benefit from the seeds in the autumn."

She was surprised he was talking to her. "My father grew mostly herbs, but they are beautiful as well, even if their flowers tend to be smaller than these royal roses," she said. She couldn't believe she had shared two sentences with Sir Richard that didn't focus on mutual animosity.

"When I'm distressed for any reason, I wander in my garden," Sir Richard explained. "When my sister passed away, I spent every day among the flowers and realized the fact of death and rebirth. It happens quite naturally in the Nature kingdom, quietly and orderly, unless a storm wreaks havoc on the tender plants."

Jill studied his face for any sign of mockery, but read only sincerity and sadness. He still struggled with his sorrow. She nodded. "It's all around us; 'tis the violence that disturbs me."

"Mayhap we live in a cruel world," he suggested, gazing at her intently.

"Yes, but there's always the other side of the coin— peace and love."

He hesitated, but he couldn't very well disagree to that, she thought. But if he wanted to argue, he would find a way.

"Yes . . . there's always that," he said with a sigh.

"But you don't believe in such romantic frills like love, do you? It's only for totty-headed females and silly greenhorns. Am I right?" She wished at the last moment that she hadn't goaded him.

"I daresay," he replied, his voice dry as dust. "I have seen more harm done in the name of love than in hate."

"Oh." She didn't know how to reply, but she sensed that he hadn't experienced an easy time in growing up. Perhaps he'd shouldered responsibility too early in life, but he seemed to thrive on it. What she'd seen of Eversley proved he took good care of everything, including the people working for him.

"Sir Richard, will you live here or at Eversley?"

"We'll have to spend time in both places until there is a male heir to take charge of the Keep. It goes in direct line to Laura's son, if she has one. Her cousin has no children."

She noted he said "she" not "we." "You're a very fortunate man, Sir Richard."

Feeling overwhelmed with a sadness she couldn't understand, she hurried farther out onto the terrace. Darkness was falling rapidly, and she couldn't see the flowers any longer but the scent filled the evening with enchantment. He didn't follow her, and it disappointed her.

Despite all the people around her, she was alone. Laura and Sir Richard had a future to plan, but she had nothing to focus on except for the dissolving of the curse. Then what?

Aunt Iddy kept urging her to find a husband, but

she hadn't met a single gentleman she found interesting. And if they were, they informed her they were married or about to be married, or they were too old. Or they thought she was odd. Sir Richard did.

With a sigh, she sipped her lemonade and realized she had to join the others, or they would wonder where she'd gone. When she entered the room, Lady Penholly was talking to Alvin, and they both looked at her, calculation in their eyes. Had he babbled the truth to her already, or would he keep his mouth shut?

"My dear, this young man says you're in possession of a fine singing voice." She held out her hand toward Jill. "I shall play later, and you'll sing, perhaps."

Jill shook her head. "He has windmills in his head. I can't keep a tune." She gave Alvin a murderous glance, and he chuckled. With a triumphant bow, he went in search of other guests—to bore no doubt, Jill thought.

Lady Penholly continued, "He whispered to me that he's quite taken with you. A nice young man. He owns a substantial estate in Devon."

Jill nodded and cursed him silently. "Be that as it may. He's made advances in the past, but I'm not interested."

"You look like someone with a lively mind, and I wish I could put my finger on what's nagging me. A man that I met in the past looked uncannily like you."

Jill wished she'd worn a blond wig or a large hat to disguise her resemblance to her father. She changed the subject. "Is your family of old Cornish lineage?"

"Oh yes, but we have a strand of Irish blood as well. But there have been Penhollys here at least five hundred years."

"You must be close to the other families in the area."

"Oh yes, I know the history in depth. You see, I always liked to study. I used to say to my mother that if I'd been a boy, I'd have been a scholar." Lady Penholly laughed. "She would get a horrified look on her face. She claims I turned peculiar because someone dropped me on my head when I was two months old."

Jill studied the guests dressed in beautiful gowns and jewelry. A long table was adorned with a white damask tablecloth and covered with a multitude of dishes from which to choose. Jill noticed strawberry tarts—the berries from the hothouse no doubt—cream cakes, chocolate éclairs, mountains of bonbons, and other sweet treats. If she tried all these, there would be no room for dinner.

"Tell me, Lady Penholly, how much do you know about the history of Endicott Keep?"

The older woman flung out her arm, and some of the wine splashed over the rim. "Lots and lots! All of its bloody past, in fact. They were a rather cruel lot, you know. It's hard to believe that Laura is part of that lineage."

"She doesn't know much about the history and has little interest in finding out more."

Lady Penholly leaned closer and lowered her voice. "And still, her life was fueled down through the ages by a witch's blood."

Jill's breath stopped in her throat and she thought she'd misheard the statement. She needed to support herself against something, but there was nothing. Taking a steadying breath, she gulped down some more lemonade. "A witch?" she croaked.

"Yes . . . the woman came from the dark forests of Eastern Europe, somewhere. It's not clear. She could've been Russian."

"Then how did she come here?"

"I doubt that she did. It's said the Endicott ancestors were traders. They traveled the world to find goods, and one of them did marry a foreigner. He must've begotten a child on the witch. She came to live at the Keep for some time the story goes, and then disappeared without a trace when her husband died. I'd say she suffered from homesickness. The Keep is not a place for someone who might be used to the deep forests of Eastern Europe."

"Mayhap she went up in smoke."

Lady Penholly laughed, that high, infectious sound. "That sounds wholly possible. She flew off to Russia on a broom and a puff of smoke."

It was Jill's turn to laugh. Here was someone who did believe in magic. "She must've left the child behind."

"A boy, and he became the carrier of that blood line." She indicated Laura with a tilt of her head. "And the pendant Laura is wearing under her lace collar was certainly dug out of the Russian wilds somewhere, possibly by the Norse."

"The markings? What are they?"

"Runes perhaps. The old Norse language, but the markings are ancient and worn. It's said to carry a power that will protect the wearer from enemies. As far as I can tell, Laura has no enemies."

"I highly doubt she has. If the story is true, there might've been enemies in the family's past." Jill longed for some evidence that the Ashcroft curse had been mentioned in the Endicott annals somewhere. "Did you learn all of this from books?" she asked, knowing the answer would be no, but she needed more.

"Laura has little interest in the past," Lady Penholly

said, "but there are accounts at the Keep. When her mother was alive—we were great friends—I used to spend time at the library there. And yes, the family had enemies in the past, an Ashcroft of Devon—pirates the lot, in the seventeenth century."

Jill's spirits sank, as she knew Lady Penholly spoke the truth. The Ashcroft ancestor had been a very bad apple on the family tree.

"The Endicotts almost lost everything as their entire shipment of goods sank to the bottom of the sea. It's one thing if someone else would've received the benefits from the ships, but no one did. A total waste it was."

"This was at the time of the witch?"

Lady Penholly nodded sagely. "She put a curse on the family of Ashcroft for all time, and as far as I know, violence and death have been that family's constant companion ever since."

"You truly believe in the curse?" Jill asked, hoping the older lady wouldn't remember Lionel Ashcroft, Jill's father.

"There's no doubt."

Relief that someone else supported her ideas came over Jill. It fueled her resolve to finally get to the bottom of this whole thing and end it.

Lady Penholly studied her thoughtfully. "You're a level-headed young woman it seems. Why are you not wed or at least betrothed?"

Jill glanced at Sir Richard, a stab of annoyance going through her. "I haven't met anyone who sparks my interest."

"Hmm. I feel Laura is rather lukewarm toward Sir Richard. He's not the right man for her."

"Lady Penholly, that's rather a bold statement."

"You only have to look at them to see that they don't suit."

Jill realized her suspicions were true—the older woman was right. Sir Richard intimidated Laura, and he needed someone with more pluck. Jill had never looked closely enough at the two to realize the truth. Not that she'd wanted to look; it truly didn't concern her.

"They're making a mammoth mistake," Lady Penholly went on. "You can't always follow the dictates of your fathers, and Sir Richard is a man of honor. He would never go back on his word, and he promised to take care of her."

"I surely would not want to spend my life fulfilling someone else's wish," Jill said.

"You're a spirited young lady, and any kind of confinement imposed upon you would surely rub you raw."

"My father allowed me a great deal of freedom," Jill said, hoping Lady Penholly wouldn't ask her about her sire. "He had rather liberal opinions for his time."

Her ladyship raised her eyebrows. "And your mother?"

"She passed on when I was very young. I barely recall."

"Ach, how hard to grow up without your mother to look after you."

"I don't remember her well enough to be plagued with longing, and my aunt has always been at my side. She never married."

"Laid down her life for her family, no doubt."

"I've never heard her complain," Jill said, realizing it was the truth. Aunt Iddy had always been the staunchest of allies.

"Hmmm . . . Iddings, the name doesn't speak to me, and I know *everybody*."

Jill trembled, thinking fast, and wondered how

knowledgeable Lady Penholly truly was. "My aunt is related to the Earl of Tregarny," she explained, which was true, but she didn't want to embroider further with that thread of ancestry.

"The Tregarnys of Devon? A more infamous lot you couldn't find."

Twelve

"Infamous?"

"Yes. . . . the gentlemen of that family were notorious—duels galore and deep gambling, and they had bad reputations with the ladies."

"That doesn't sound like any relative of my aunt," Jill said defensively. At least Lady Penholly hadn't brought up the Ashcrofts again. If she knew the Iddings, she might know their connection.

But the lady trilled a greeting to some new guests and excused herself. Jill drew a sigh of relief. All she had to do now was to stay away from Alvin, duck Sir Richard and his accusations, and generally make herself invisible. With a plate of tiny cakes, she went to find a seat outside on the terrace.

In these cakes she would find heaven—temporarily.

Laura joined her shortly, her face somewhat pale. Perspiration pearled on her forehead. Julian followed closely on her heels.

She sat down with a sigh and glanced at Jill's plate.

"I don't know how you can eat in this close weather. I fear a thunderstorm is coming." She fanned herself with a painted vellum fan, her lips drooping downward at the corners, and her shoulders slumping.

Jill dabbed at her mouth with a napkin. "You look rather green around the gills."

Julian said, "She has been rather distraught, and

she won't confide in me." He patted Laura's shoulder. "You always used me as your confidant."

Laura shot him a quick glance, and Jill saw the confusion in her eyes. Jill addressed Julian. "Would you fetch a glass of water for her?"

"Certainly."

When he left, Jill put down her plate and ordered Laura to lie down on the wooden bench. Laura obeyed, throwing one arm across her eyes.

Jill took her own fan and fluttered it over Laura's face. "What's the matter?"

Laura sighed. "I don't know, but I. . . . Sir Richard kissed me in the garden this morning . . . and—" Her voice petered out.

"Did he frighten you?"

Laura shook her head, but her eyes looked haunted when she lifted up her arm. "No . . . but I'm not sure I want him to kiss me again. Ever."

"It was that awful?" Jill recalled the heated explosion she'd felt under the pressure of Sir Richard's mouth on hers, and guilt overcame her.

Laura nodded. "Well, yes, and he kept fiddling with my necklace."

Jill froze. "Are you certain? It might just have been the way he held you that put pressure on it."

Laura made a grimace. "I don't know; it just didn't feel right. This is all happening too fast."

"Surely you can speak to Sir Richard about this?"

"Just the thought of bringing it up makes me more sick to the stomach." She groaned exaggeratedly.

Jill sat down and loosened the lace collar around Laura's neck. There the Endicott pendant beckoned and mocked at the same time, and Jill silently gritted her teeth. With her napkin, she patted Laura's forehead.

The air did feel close; the atmosphere had shifted completely, and Jill sensed the restless clouds rolling in. "You were right about the weather."

"I always am, you know. Thunder affects me strangely."

Jill stared mesmerized at the pendant. It seemed to glow this evening as if responding to the oppressive weather. She reached out and placed the tip of her index finger on it, and Laura jerked.

She stared curiously at Jill. "What did you do?"

"I . . . I touched the pendant just to feel the stone," Jill replied weakly.

Julian returned with the water, and Laura sat back up and rearranged the lace at her throat. "Everyone seems so interested in my pendant lately. No one ever took an interest before."

"It's a curious piece."

"I always wondered about that," Julian said and sat down next to Laura and placed a protective arm around her. He held out the water glass, and Laura took it gratefully.

"Thank you."

Jill wished he would go away so that she could continue her conversation with Laura, but Julian didn't leave their side. Before long, thunder boomed in the distance, and Jill remembered that Cornwall was known for its violent storms. This was the kind of night when wreckers in the past had lured ships to go aground upon the jagged rocks of the coast so that they could plunder the goods.

Laura looked a little better as the storm burst, sending sheets of water across the terrace. They hurried inside and footmen closed the doors against the gusting winds. Lightning slashed across the black sky and thunder rolled ominously.

Sir Richard came across the room to Laura's side, but Julian didn't let go of his grip on her elbow.

"My dear," Sir Richard said and took Laura's other elbow. "Are you unwell? Do you want to return home?"

"And ruin the evening for everyone else? No, I cannot do that." She patted her hair, which had been made into ringlets and gathered at the top of her head. "I'm feeling much better." She touched Julian's arm. "Thanks to you, my friend. And you," she added, turning to Jill.

Thunder rolled again, sullen and drawn out as if to remind them of the power of elements.

Filled with frustration, Jill wondered if she ever would have a chance to nab the Endicott pendant.

She found no opportunity at all during the next few days, and her and Aunt Iddy's stay was coming to an end. According to the legend, the pendant would have to be buried at Lindenwood during the night of a full moon, which would happen the following week. If she were ever to get the pendant, it would have to happen within the next few days.

Sir Richard evidently shared her frustration. She came in contact with him one morning as she sat reading at the lookout point above the cliffs. Had he come to argue with her? She gave him an intent stare but didn't notice anything out of the ordinary. In fact he looked rather ill at ease.

To her surprise, he sat down on the bench beside her. "Good morning," he greeted, his voice glum.

She responded in kind. "Why so Friday-faced?"

She thought he would deny it, but he looked even grimmer if possible. If it hadn't been for the dark expression, she would have admired his handsome profile and gleaming hair.

He looked elegant in a coat of blue superfine, pantaloons, and Hessians. It took only a few seconds for her to realize he wore the clothes of a metropolis gent, not a country squire.

"I'm leaving for a few days, but I'll have you know I tried again to steal Laura's pendant," he said.

Breathless, she waited for an explanation.

"I crept into her room when she was taking her bath behind some screens. I saw the pendant on her dressing table, but the abigail stood right there, with her back toward me, and it's a great fortune that she didn't discover me. It would've raised an uproar."

Jill knew he had made a tremendous effort to help her. "Thank you." She didn't know why, but she had the strangest urge to touch him. Laying a hand on his back as he leaned forward, she added, "I am grateful for your attempts."

"You can't stay here much longer," he added.

She nodded. "I know." They were lost in the moment of mutual awareness as they gazed at each other.

"You might not succeed."

"It looks rather impossible at the moment, but I shan't leave without the pendant." Jill spoke with conviction, and sensed the fight within him. She rose to stand by the balustrade.

The view of the sea spread out before her in a quilt of various greens and blues, and the waves ate restlessly at the base of the massive black rocks below. The same agitation moved within her. She lived on the tip of one of those jagged rocks, and one wrong move would topple her.

He came to stand beside her and leaned his arms on the railing. "I admire your tenacity, but I'm also deathly tired of this charade. It's bordering on the ridiculous."

"To me it isn't. I abhor the fact that I'm deceiving Laura, but what choice do I have?" She knew she sounded peevish. She'd never felt so frustrated.

He didn't reply, only stared at her, making her uncomfortable. Acutely aware of his proximity, she longed to feel his arms around her, but at the same time she wanted to flee as panic overtook her.

She could never allow herself any desires for Sir Richard, nor could she expect him to help her further. When all was said and done, he had helped her a great deal already.

"I'm grateful," she said, after taking a deep breath, "for your assistance so far. Without you, I would never have gotten to this point."

He laughed. "My guess is you would've found a way. You have the tenacity of a terrier."

"That sounds ominous somehow."

He shook his head. "No, it's a great quality for accomplishing the impossible."

She gazed out to sea. "So you believe it's impossible?"

"Yes, I do."

"It cannot be. There has to be a way."

"I don't see it unless you actually cut off the chain while someone holds Laura down."

Now it was her turn to laugh. "Are you a willing accomplice?"

He snorted in outrage. "No, absolutely not! She may never forgive me. *You* she will never ever forgive when she learns of your deception, but I have a spotless reputation so far. If she discovers my part, she might not forgive me either."

"Wouldn't that be a shame," she chided.

His gaze narrowed as he looked at her, and nervous laughter bubbled in her throat.

He groaned. "You have the temerity to joke about my precarious position?"

"Jesting is the only way I can keep myself sane."

"You don't know the meaning of the word," he said, and she wondered if he truly meant it.

His lips twitched and she longed to kick him, but she didn't move as his eyes glittered dangerously. Her heartbeat escalated alarmingly and her emotions felt as if they were about to choke her. The moment stretched eternally between them, and he closed the distance without taking his eyes off her. She heard a whimper in her throat as he leaned over her. His warm hands cupped her face, and before she could find her voice to protest, he kissed her.

The fiery pressure of his mouth on hers made her soar, and she kissed him back with a passion that surprised her. He was the first man who had awakened these kinds of feelings within her.

She clung to him knowing she would fall if he didn't hold her. He held her so tightly she thought she would dissolve into him. She forgot about everything except the warm pressure of his mouth.

When he released his hold, she stumbled backward into the balustrade. If it hadn't been there, she would've fallen. She steadied herself and touched her lips that still tingled from his pressure.

A cloud of guilt moved across his face, and he dropped his hands to his sides as if they were lead weights. "I . . . I'm so very sorry," he said hoarsely. "I have no idea what came over me."

She swallowed hard, her throat dry. "Yes, you do," she croaked. "You had an impulse to kiss me, for whatever reason, and you did. Mayhap you remembered the last time."

"The last time?"

"When you kissed me."

He looked away and she knew that another wave of guilt engulfed him. He didn't reply.

She sighed and patted her arrangement of curls to make sure they still sat demurely gathered. "We shouldn't be here unchaperoned."

"That would never bother you, Jill."

"But it might you, and you don't seem to mind pushing your advances on me."

He bowed. "You're correct, and if you had a supportive male relative, he would call me out for what I just did."

"And run you through, no doubt." She shook her head and laughed. "It's the outside of enough. For this you're now lumped together with all the womanizers in town—in my humble opinion."

"And you know who they are? You have personal knowledge of these gentlemen?" he goaded.

She pinched her lips together and gave him a withering stare.

His shoulders slumped. "You're right." He kicked the toe of his boot against the bottom of the balustrade. "For some reason I find it very difficult to feel a romantic spark for Laura."

"You believe in love, then?" she whispered.

She sensed the turmoil going through him. "I never thought much of it."

Until now, she wanted to add, but said nothing.

"I certainly don't expect to fall in love with someone my father chose as my bride. That's a given. Cupid's arrow rarely touches arranged marriages."

She nodded. "You're right, but that doesn't mean you might not come to love Laura in due time."

He sounded frustrated. "I *do* love her, like a brother would love a sister."

"Yes. . . ." For some reason the information made her happy, but guilt gnawed away at her constantly. His not loving Laura didn't mean she, Jill, would reside in his heart. Besides, he would never go back on his pledge.

Just imagine if Sir Richard would fall in love with her. She would never be able to face Laura again. Not only would she have stolen the pendant; she would've stolen Laura's intended husband.

It just wouldn't do.

"Under no circumstances can you touch me again," she said. "I shan't speak of this to Laura, because I'm as guilty as you are, but we can't ever repeat these kinds of actions and live with ourselves."

He nodded curtly. "Thank you for your understanding." He made as if to move down the path, but stopped right in front of her. He lifted his hand and pushed a stray curl behind her ear, but the breeze fluttered it right back across her face.

"I promise it'll never happen again," he said, his voice rough as if he had difficulty expressing the words.

Without another word, she rushed down the path, her skirts swishing against the gorse that grew alongside.

Sir Richard looked after her, his heart feeling tight in his chest. All these strange emotions upset him, and he had difficulty understanding why they clamored in his chest. His heart squeezed even further as he recalled every nuance of her dark eyes and that unruly hair that always seemed to be on the verge of tumbling down.

Her passion for life had infected him somehow and he needed her *joie de vivre;* it made him feel alive. She made him forget his sorrow.

He would have to file these weeks away as the strangest in his life, marry Laura, and forget that Jill ever existed. If Jill got any further under his skin, he knew he would end up totally miserable.

Thirteen

Sir Richard left the Keep and Jill wanted to cry with longing. His absence had created a huge hole in her heart, it seemed.

When he returned three days later, she yearned to throw herself into his arms, but he only gave her a curt nod, unwilling to spend any time at all with her. Her frustration grew unbearable, and there was no one she could talk to. Everyone would look at her as a traitor. Her insides in turmoil, tears poured down her cheeks, but she wiped them away in seclusion. It wouldn't do to have Aunt Iddy find her with red eyes and a swollen nose. She would ask a slew of uncomfortable questions, and Jill could not answer them.

If she didn't gather her wits, she would be undone, jeopardizing her whole mission. No gentleman was worthy of such bitter tears, she thought.

Julian, Viscount Sandhurst, had invited them all to a dinner party. When the night at Sandhurst arrived, he greeted them at the door. The square old sandstone mansion built in the seventeenth century glowed golden in the failing sunlight, and the deep mullioned windows seemed to hold secrets in their shadows.

Old roses climbed up the walls, softening the plain lines of the stone. The park had been manicured and lilacs blossomed, sending out a sweet, intoxicating scent. The stillness of the evening was in sharp contrast to the chatting guests.

Jill almost followed the urge to disappear in the garden for a moment, but Julian kept pushing everyone forward, and when she saw Edgar talking to Alvin in the front parlor, she filled with fear.

What was *he* doing here? Edgar must've invited him to dinner.

Aunt Iddy looked startled as well, her cheeks reddening, and Jill noticed the trembling of her hands. This charade was taking a toll on her aunt.

Alvin gave them a smile that reminded Jill of the cat that got into the cream. She stared at him in challenge, and he bowed exaggeratedly in her direction. She fully expected him to rush across the room with the words "dear Coz" loud and clear, but he bided his time, taking in the scene around him. He bowed to Aunt Iddy and Laura's aunt as well.

Jill gave Aunt Iddy a glance that warned her to keep quiet, and her long-suffering relative, not one to excel in subterfuge, fled to the adjoining chamber, pulling Penelope with her.

The mansion had been decorated with old tapestries and plaster busts, portraits, and Oriental urns. Everywhere Jill looked she noticed soothing jewel colors of deep reds and blues, browns and dark greens. Some of the diamond-shaped panes of the windows were stained glass, which created their own colored light as the evening sunlight slanted through them.

"This is a lovely old home," Jill said to Julian and Laura who stood beside her.

"Yes, I always wanted to live here as the master of the estate," Julian said.

Jill thought it was a strange reply coming from someone who knew he would someday be Viscount

Sandhurst, but perhaps he meant that Sandhurst had always been important to him.

"I love this old heap," Laura said. She looked beautiful in a white silk Empire gown embroidered with rose buds. Roses had been pinned in her hair, and that cursed pendant adorned her neck. "I always did. It's not fierce and rugged like the Keep. It's like a refined old dowager." She turned to Julian. "Just like your grandmother." She stared up the carved staircase as if expecting to see the old lady. "How is she?"

"She rarely leaves her rooms," Julian said.

"I'd like to see her."

"No need," he said curtly. "Don't disappoint yourself. She would not recognize you."

Laura made a *moue*. "She was always kind to me."

Jill looked at Julian, noticing the handsome lines of his face and the noble curve of his nose. He gave Laura a dazzling smile, and Laura's cheeks blossomed. Was it possible that Cupid's arrow had truly struck in that direction? Jill wondered, and only wished happiness for Laura.

The turmoil Jill felt every time she looked at her friend was making life very difficult.

When Laura took her bath tomorrow, the pendant would disappear. It was the only course left to Jill. Laura refused to even discuss the pendant anymore.

Jill sent a glance in Sir Richard's direction. He had avoided looking at her since he returned, possibly remembering their last encounter by the balustrade, and she tried to avoid him at all cost. Riding with him in the carriage to Sandhurst had been an ordeal.

Laura hadn't noticed his taciturn demeanor, but Aunt Iddy had stared at him through her thick glasses and fluttered her fan as if full of worry.

We have to leave without delay, Jill thought. Time was definitely running out; she was sitting on a keg of gunpowder.

They all went in to dinner. Laura sat by Julian at the head of the table while Sir Richard sat straight across. He didn't say much, and looked as if he wanted to strangle someone.

Jill sat between Alvin and Edgar, and *she* definitely wanted to strangle them both or push their faces into the bowls of clear beef broth set before them.

Edgar's shirt points kept stabbing him in the cheeks, and Alvin blabbered on how he would win at the horse races even if he had lost a minor fortune at the card tables only yesterday. He would lose money just sitting at a table staring straight ahead, Jill thought. He always had pockets to let.

"I shall marry someone—a beauty—with a great deal of money," Edgar announced to Jill in his nasal tones. "Not just anyone will do," he continued as if warning Jill that she had no chances in his direction even if she did have funds.

"'Tis hard to find a combination of both, perhaps," Jill said coolly.

"Not for me. I have a kind of allure that women can't resist," he went on, and this time, Jill was truly appalled.

"I daresay it's the soap you're using," she said blandly.

He looked at her as if shocked. "'Tis not seemly to talk about such intimate details as soap," he scolded, looking down his blade of a nose. "Your upbringing has much to be desired, Miss Iddings."

"I can't say I'm impressed with your social skills either," she said between gritted teeth, and Alvin kicked her in the leg under the table.

Frankly, I know I'm above reproach, and I have never heard anyone complain about my graces before."

That's because you can't see beyond the sharp tip of your nose, Jill thought uncharitably. *Or hear anyone else's voice besides your own.*

She didn't reply and he turned to Aunt Iddy on his other side, immediately harassing her. Fortunately, Aunt Iddy wasn't argumentative tonight, Jill thought. Too nervous.

"You're playing a rum game," Alvin said under his breath. "I shall get to the bottom of it. You can't bury yourself in this godforsaken hole forever." He squeezed her elbow and leaned very close, and she saw that Sir Richard had noticed the maneuver. He scowled, and she suspected he thought she was egging Alvin on. A pox take the man, she thought, meaning both of them. They caused nothing but difficulties and emotional turmoil.

"I'm very curious; you have to explain yourself, Coz, or I'll ask everyone what you're about," Alvin hissed in her ear. A spray of spittle flew across her cheek, and she longed to shout at him to stay away, but had to manage a stiff smile.

"Go back to the Metropolis, Alvin." She tore her arm away from his touch.

"I won't leave until you give me some answers, Coz."

"Don't call me 'Coz'."

"Don't keep any secrets from me, Coz. Someone knows everything." He gave Aunt Iddy a pointed look, and Jill froze with fear. Aunt Iddy was no match for Alvin.

"Very well, I'll tell you something," Jill replied. "I want the pendant that Laura wears all the time."

He threw a quick glance at the Endicott pendant as Laura leaned forward to better hear something Julian was saying. "Oh, that. I don't understand why, but when a female gets an idea into her head there's usually no stopping her."

"Balderdash! I resent your opinion of myself and my fair sisters."

"I could give you any number of necklaces that would be prettier than that," he replied scornfully. "It has absolutely nothing to recommend itself."

Jill made a quick decision to explain about its power. "I know your father and mine weren't close and that we didn't see each other much until these later years," she began in a low voice. "If you remember, my father dabbled in a number of metaphysical studies, among them astrology."

"I recall. He was considered a madman, and very stubborn. You're too much like him, and I don't find it attractive." Alvin glowered, but she forged ahead.

"He knew a lot more than you ever will, Alvin," she said, glaring back. "Your father died in a shooting accident, and you must've heard the Ashcroft curse mentioned at that time."

"That silly business again! I've never believed for one moment that the legend had any grain of truth."

"Well, I believe, and I'm about to save your sorry hide, whether you want it or not. For that, I need the pendant."

"I still don't understand the connection."

"You don't have to, Alvin. Let me take care of it, but don't you tattle; if you do, we're both lost."

He snorted so loudly that everyone looked up. Jill tensed, wondering if he would say something, but he only smiled his detestable ingratiating smile and everyone continued his or her conversation, all except Sir Richard who gave her a narrow stare. Drat the man! His mistrust galled her.

"Alvin, you have to promise—"

"By Jupiter, you are as cork-brained as your father! I thought you were only a little unconventional, but the roots go a lot deeper, don't they?"

"You are a walking monument of arrogance, Alvin." Anger rose hot in her chest, and she had to fight an urge to march from the room. "But I don't care what you *think* as long as you don't *do* anything. Just stay away from me."

"You're not the only Ashcroft who has a stubborn streak," he said. "I shall let you lead me into parson's mousetrap without delay."

"You're wearing me to a shade," she whispered. "I have told you countless times that I have no desire to wed you. If I were penniless you wouldn't as much as look in my direction."

"Well, you have a point there. It's not as if your colors are fashionable; you're too dark and too intense. Fair Laura is more in the way of popular taste."

"You're the most thoughtless individual I've ever met, and I'm sorry to call you 'cousin.' You and Edgar are cut from the same cloth, and I pray that you'll never find wives to torture with your selfishness." At this point, Jill almost had to leave the room to vent her anger, but she only gritted her teeth. She didn't want any attention directed at her.

Knowing it would gall her no end, Alvin bestowed a kiss on her hand. She snatched it away and glowered at him.

The main dish consisted of a rack of lamb with mint sauce and tiny potatoes. Everything tasted like sawdust after her confrontation with Alvin. Even the massive chocolate cake with whipped cream tasted less than perfect. Everyone else seemed to eat with gusto, but her stomach gnawed with worry.

After dinner, she took a stroll in the garden with the two aunts and they commented on the profusion of peonies, blooming in different shades of pink and red. A knot garden of herbs sent out wisps of sweet scents and bumblebees droned among the flowers. The last of the evening sun spread a golden tone over everything, and Jill would have enjoyed it if she hadn't been so upset.

She prayed Alvin would do nothing to ruin her mission, but she couldn't dissolve the knot of tension in her stomach.

When she returned inside after leaving the aunts chatting on a garden bench, she accidentally walked through the French doors leading to the library rather than the front parlor. She came upon Laura and Julian embracing and deeply engaged in a kiss. They jumped apart as they heard her, both wearing guilty expressions. Laura blushed to the roots of her hair and tried to push Julian away.

"Oh . . . I'm sorry," Jill mumbled, and turned as if to leave.

"Don't go," Laura called out, her voice trembling.

As Jill faced her, she sent an imploring glance at Julian who bowed and left the room, closing the door softly behind him.

"I didn't mean to intrude," Jill said hesitantly.

"I know." Laura came to Jill's side and pulled her to a cushioned seat built under the mullioned window. They sat down together.

"Were you two . . . kissing?"

Laura's face flushed anew. "I've always had a *tendre* for Julian, but he's never looked at me as more than a sister, until recently."

"When Sir Richard appeared on the scene."

"It has always been known that I am betrothed to

Richard, but the fact has not been real until lately. My nuptials are soon, too soon."

"You're regretting the match," Jill probed, feeling both disturbed and hopeful. *If Laura didn't want Sir Richard she wouldn't mind if he turned to Jill, would she?*

Laura nodded, her face wreathed in misery. "I don't think we would suit. Sir Richard—"

"Is a rather commanding fellow," Jill filled in.

"Yes. . . . I like him, but he doesn't touch my heart."

"Then you have to tell him."

"He will be so very angry with me. This was something he promised his father."

"Promises like that should not be fulfilled by force. Your heart is more important than his temper." Jill paused. "And Julian? Has he declared himself?"

"Well . . . not exactly. But it's all so new and tender." Laura squeezed Jill's hand. "What if Richard challenges Julian to a duel?"

Jill thought it could be a probable outcome. "You have to talk sense into him, make him understand that he's not bound to the promises in any way, that if it hadn't been for your fathers, you would never have considered marriage to him."

Laura clapped her hands to her warm cheeks. "'Tis so very difficult."

"Sometimes we have to face troublesome issues with fortitude."

"Yes . . . I know."

"Laura, has Julian indicated any of his feelings verbally?" Jill asked. She remembered his cynical demeanor at a different dinner table.

"Yes—no, not exactly, but I sense what he feels, and he can't always find the right words. He's somewhat shy."

"Hmm, shy? I doubt it. I find him rather a smooth

fellow, not one lacking expression or Town bronze. He's not a greenhorn, nor is he very open." It surprised Jill that Laura didn't see his suave manner, but her friend had little experience in the ways of the world.

"He whispered the most romantic nonsense to me," Laura confessed, a new wave of pink washing over her face.

A sense of unease came over Jill. Laura's confession disturbed her; she had to wonder if Julian could be trusted. After all, he was an extremely handsome gentleman who would be used to the admiration of the ladies. In contrast to Sir Richard, he had an easy charm, but how deep did it go? Jill couldn't answer that, as she didn't know him well enough. She also remembered that he'd greeted Lady Penholly with great familiarity that might speak of more than mere friendship.

"You'll need to think about this, Laura. Don't make any hasty decisions." Jill gathered her friend into her arms and held her. The confusion was contagious. Jill couldn't trust her own feelings for Sir Richard, but she trusted his honor.

"You have to make sure Julian is truly the right man for you, not just some object of your infatuation."

As she hugged Laura, the pendant bounced against her shoulder and she could feel a current going through her. When Laura pulled away, Jill couldn't help herself as she reached over and held the pendant between her fingertips.

"I so admire this," she whispered. "Would you accept a monetary offer for it?"

"No!"

Laura snatched the pendant away. "I don't understand why everyone seems to have this sudden obsession with my heirloom. I can understand your admiration, but not Sir Richard's. That he would be interested in acquiring it boggles my mind."

"He appreciates old things," Jill said feebly.

"He hasn't tried to purchase it," Laura explained. "Only you have." She looked curiously at her friend. "I have to confess I find it rather odd."

"Don't pay any heed to me."

"You are my friend."

Jill's heart hammered in her chest. If only she could explain the truth. But if she did, would Laura banish her in anger? If she did, the hope of dispelling the curse would be lost forever. "I appreciate your friendship more than you know, Laura." And that was the truth, but how could she gain the pendant?

There was only one thing left to do; she had hoped it wouldn't come to this, but she had to face the truth. She had to steal it when Laura took her bath.

Fourteen

Sir Richard stared at Jill as she explained her last desperate plan that night after they had returned to the Keep. She had pulled him out onto the terrace when everyone else had retired.

"I believe this is my only chance. I found out that Laura ordered hot water for tomorrow morning. This is my opportunity; I was so reluctant to face the fact that I have to steal it, but I have no choice."

He shook his head, his expression grim. "I can't be involved in your schemes any longer. If you steal—or if you fail—don't count on my support."

For a moment, a cold loneliness came over her, but she pushed it aside. Some things were more important than silly yearnings of her heart.

"Yes, I know."

"Why are you telling me this?" he demanded. "I'd prefer to be in blissful ignorance about your plans for tomorrow."

"I understand," she said with a sigh. She didn't know why she'd felt a need to tell him. Perhaps she longed for some understanding, for support. Aunt Iddy sustained her, but she hadn't done anything to help Jill execute her mission.

"I can't and won't help you."

"I'm aware of that, so there's no need to repeat it," she said crossly. Possibly she wouldn't see him again after tomorrow. As soon as she had the pendant, she would return to Lindenwood and bury it at the spot where the curse would be broken. "I shall leave and you won't have to concern yourself with my business further."

He remained silent, and she was grateful for it.

She gazed at him and he looked at her as if they could not tear themselves away.

"I suppose it's time to go upstairs now and seek some rest," she said lamely.

He nodded. "That's what you do after a full day." His sardonic smile didn't make her feel better. Just the thought that she might not see him again made her sad.

"Tell me," he said, "have you noticed anything different in Laura?"

"In what sense?"

"She seems . . . well, withdrawn. I believe she deliberately hides from me."

"I don't know," Jill said cautiously. "Laura will have to speak for herself."

"She hasn't spoken to you?"

Jill hated to tell him an outright lie, but this matter had nothing to do with her. "You need to approach Laura, not me."

He sighed and she could read the frustration on his face. "It's . . . well . . . easier to talk to you," he said lamely.

"Fiddlesticks," she scoffed. "We do nothing but argue."

"At least I know what to expect from you, Jill, and I have no problem handling it."

She laughed. "Of all the paltry things to say! I've had quite enough of you."

His eyes held a stormy expression, challenging her.

"Have you?" He took a step closer and gripped her arms. An intoxicating scent of lilacs filled the night, and Jill thought she would swoon with the intensity of his gaze upon her.

She gasped as he leaned closer, pulling her tight. Her whimper of protest died on her lips as he kissed her with passion, a demanding, warm touch that set her blood tingling through her veins. How could this be happening—again?

She tore herself away with great reluctance. "You're trifling with me," she said, her voice trembling.

He shook his head. "No, I don't know what comes over me when I'm alone with you. Either we're at loggerheads, or I have an irresistible urge to kiss you and hold you tight."

"You have to control your urges, or I'll make sure that Laura finds out about your perfidy."

"I'm sorry," he said, but she could read no repentance in his expression. They had both enjoyed the romantic gesture, and she was appalled to find out that she wanted more of his attention. How could she have turned to such a state of debauchery? It was the outside of enough to lead Laura behind the light about her true reason for visiting the Keep, but to kiss Laura's fiancé in the dark bordered on criminal.

"I can't do this, Richard." He'd remained standing close to her, and she pushed him away. "Everything ends here. I'll be gone from the Keep shortly, and you shall marry Laura."

"Plague take it," he swore under his breath, then apologized for his language.

"I cannot continue to stay here," Jill continued.

He shook his head. "No, you can't. If you steal the pendant tomorrow morning, the truth will come out, and you won't be welcome here any longer."

"So I leave tomorrow," she said simply and walked away. Every step was an effort, and she wondered if he experienced the same longing she harbored for him. With every step another tear gathered in her eyes, but she had to remain strong. This stay at the Keep had been such a nightmare. She almost wished she'd never set eyes on Sir Richard.

"Good night," she heard his voice behind her, but she didn't reply.

After an almost sleepless night, she got up very early. Laura wouldn't be up for a couple of hours yet. Surely she slept peacefully without any kind of concern for her pendant. Jill dressed in her riding habit and decided to take some exercise to blow the cobwebs from her mind. A bundle of trembling nerves, she knew she had to do something or go mad.

She tied the ribbons of her hat under her chin and sought her gloves. With her boots in her hand, she tiptoed along the corridor, not wishing to awaken anyone. For a moment she stopped outside Laura's door. What if Laura had done the unthinkable and taken off the pendant for the night?

Her hands started sweating as she pulled the door ajar. It opened on quiet hinges, thank God. She peered into the gloom, noticing that the bed hangings had been pulled closed. The abigail slept in a trundle bed under one of the windows, snoring.

Very cautiously, Jill went inside and looked on the dressing table, but found no sign of the pendant. She glanced at the nightstand, but it was too dark to tell whether Laura had put anything on top.

No pendant in sight.

Her heart thundered with fear, and she took a look

at the surface of a dresser and a round table, but
sensed that Laura had not removed the pendant from
her neck.

Holding her breath, Jill sneaked out of the room. If
only it could've been that easy, but the struggle for obtaining the pendant continued.

The air outside still held the cool of the night. Dew
lay thick over the grounds and hung on every leaf in
the trees. A jackdaw flew, startled out of an elm, cawing.

She would've enjoyed the morning if her heart
hadn't weighed so heavily in her chest. She would attain
her goal and then this whole charade would be over. In
time she would forget Sir Richard, but it would be difficult. He would never be hers, and she wasn't sure if
she would feel that kind of passion ever again.

Tears stung her eyes, but she wiped them away with
an angry swipe of her hand. Don't be a romantic fool,
she told herself.

The stable grooms had already accomplished many
of their morning chores. The horses munched on hay
in their stalls and turned placid eyes on Jill as she
walked up to the mare that had served her earlier. She
asked one of the grooms to saddle the spirited horse,
and he complied, giving her surreptitious stares. They
all probably wondered why she had risen so early and
desired a solitary ride.

She rode along the ridge, past Sandhurst and down
through the village of Pendenny. She remembered
the witch who had seen the dark cloud around her.
She sighed, thinking that cloud surely had grown
denser with everything that had happened lately.

Deceit never served any purpose, and for a moment she didn't care if she ever succeeded with her
mission. She could just continue to ride East toward
Devon and no one would be the wiser.

Stop feeling sorry for yourself, you silly goose! Of course she wouldn't give up, not when she'd gone along this far.

To her surprise, she found Alvin outside the local inn where he'd stopped to let his horse drink from the water trough. She wished he hadn't seen her, but he already had. An unpleasant smile spread across his face.

"Coz, what an unexpected delight."

She reined in the mare. "To be up this early, you must've committed some devilry," she replied.

"Far from it. Spent the night at card games with one of Sandhurst's neighbors, and won five hundred pounds."

He did look extraordinarily pleased, she thought. "Well, then you can pay back some of your debts."

He looked aghast. "Pay? Whatever for? The tailors and the merchants are encroaching mushrooms and should be kept in their place."

"For that, I ought to just let the curse continue until it finishes you off," she said. "You're a shabster of the worst kind, a regular cod's head, a loose fish, a counter-coxcomb, an oaf, and a lout."

"I will not wrangle with you this early," he replied with a grimace of disgust.

"Some creditor might kill you before the curse does, and I wouldn't blame them one bit," she replied, feeling quite uncharitable.

"You still go on about that nonsense of the Ashcroft curse?"

"'Tis not nonsense, Alvin."

He shrugged, but she sensed his unease. Last night he'd taken a look at Laura's pendant on the sly, but had made no comment to Jill about it.

"You're a complete goosecap, Jill, but I'm still willing to have you."

"So that you can run through my inheritance before the year is up? Hardly."

He gave her a malevolent glare, but she'd never feared him. She always stood up to bullies, and as long as she could remember she'd been at odds with Alvin.

"You'll come to me soon enough," he said with careless conviction. "I know how much you love Lindenwood."

"Not that much," she replied heatedly. "Even if I can never set foot there again, I shall be content. There are too many sad memories at Lindenwood."

"You're talking gammon, Jill."

"You never lived there until now, so you don't know the half of it. When strange things begin to happen to you, don't approach me."

He turned away from her and gripped the reins of his horse. "I've heard enough. You always come carrying gloom, and I for one, have no desire to listen."

Jill urged her mare to move along the path. When she peered over her shoulder, she noticed that Alvin had gone in the opposite direction. She drew a sigh of relief.

Good riddance.

She debated whether to ride through the small forest, and decided against it. The morning was beautiful and the moor beckoned. Its harsh beauty had surprised her. This morning the grass was rife with activity. Rabbits bounded across her path, and birds twittered and foraged in the clumps of bushes along the edge of the moor.

Her horse moved around the stand of gorse and to Jill's surprise she found an old woman all dressed in gray sitting on a grassy mound. She so blended in with her surroundings that Jill hadn't seen her at first.

She should've known she could not avoid the witch,

and she realized that part of her had wanted to see the old woman again.

The witch leaned on her gnarled walking stick, her face a pale oval in the folds of her hood that protected her from the wind blowing across the moor.

"I was waiting for you," Tula said, her voice raspy and ancient.

"I'm surprised," Jill said, but she wasn't.

"That's a plumper if I ever heard one." She gave Jill a long hard look. "You're playing with a dangerous legacy, but you're about to have your wish. The curse is very powerful."

Jill's heartbeat escalated. Here was someone at last who believed her! "You know about it, but didn't talk to me about it?"

"It binds you to a dark past, always has. Much anger and vitriol was put into the spell, but you have a fire that matches *hers*, that old tormentor of the family."

Jill nodded, tears flooding to her eyes. "You don't know how relieved I am that you know of my struggle."

"You cannot hide behind untruths and deception any longer. The daughter of the Endicott Keep needs to be brought into the secret so that it can be successfully dissolved."

"She will abhor me."

"Not as much as you hate yourself for deceiving her."

Jill pondered that and knew the witch spoke the truth. "Do you know about Lucinda the Evil?"

"Only that of which the legends speak, but I sense her power still, that's how strong she was—but in a negative way, which today has her still writhing in her grave. When love is turned into vengeance, it's returned tenfold and she had no knowledge of that. All she brought was suffering upon herself—and others."

Jill nodded, again relieved that someone could see her point. She hadn't dreamt it all.

"Go back to the Keep now. I shall hold you in my prayers. You're the savior of your family, just remember that."

Jill thanked the old woman and gave her a purse of coins. The witch gave her a pouch filled with a powdery substance.

"Wear this around your neck for protection. You'll need it."

Jill did as she was told. The pouch smelled awful as if something dead had been left inside, but she didn't dare to comment and she trusted in the witch's wisdom.

Jill could be strong now, no matter what happened.

She rode back in high spirits and entered the hallway in time to hear a wild scream from the upstairs bedrooms.

Heart in her throat, she ran toward the sound. Another shriek came, obviously from Laura's bedchamber.

On the landing, Sir Richard joined her. He must've spent the night in one of the guest bedchambers, and he still wore last night's clothes. He looked haggard as if he hadn't slept any more than she had.

A few steps behind him stormed the two aunts. They reached the door at the same time.

Jill knocked frantically. "Laura, what—?"

The door was flung open and Laura came out, still in her dressing gown. A waft of rose soap exited with her. She looked frantic, and Jill took both of her hands.

"My pendant is gone! I put it on my dressing table when I went to take a bath. Lottie went to fetch a freshly laundered gown from downstairs, and I heard my door open and close. I thought she'd come back."

"Have you looked everywhere?" Jill asked. "It might've fallen behind the dressing table." She gave Sir Richard a questioning glance. He frowned and shook his head. Evidently he hadn't stolen it, and neither had she.

But she knew who had—Alvin.

Tears started rolling down Laura's cheeks and she wiped them off with the back of her hand. "We looked there, but it couldn't have walked away on its own."

Everyone listened in silence, and then Sir Richard stepped unbidden into the room and started searching under pillows and all across the floor. An Oriental carpet covered most of it, and its pattern could very well hide a simple gray stone.

The aunts and Jill joined the search as Lottie stood wringing her hands in despair. Laura sat on the edge of a chair, dejected.

"I *know* someone took it. All of a sudden, everyone shows an interest in my pendant. It's *mine* not someone else's, and it's an ancient family heirloom that I would never part with voluntarily." She heaved a huge trembling sob. "I just don't understand it."

Sir Richard stopped his search and stared beseechingly at Jill, who felt dread rising from the pit of her stomach. She glanced at the aunts, flitting about looking for the pendant, and then there was poor Lottie who would have to shoulder the blame even if Laura didn't reprimand her.

Jill went to sit next to Laura on the chaise-longue. "I think I know what happened." She looked back at Sir Richard who stood in the middle of the room, frowning.

Laura's eyes grew huge. "You do?"

Jill's heart beat so hard that she could barely get the

words out. Silently, she cursed her trembling voice. "I'm afraid I know who took the pendant."

"Who?"

"My cousin—Alvin Ashcroft." She turned to Lottie. "Will you please fetch Brumley so that we can verify this?"

Lottie curtsied and left the room in a flurry.

"Ashcroft?" Laura had paled and her eyes looked too huge for her face. "The name of the people who almost destroyed our family?"

Jill nodded, feeling faint with worry. "I'm Jillian Ashcroft, not Iddings." She gestured toward Aunt Iddy. "She is truly my aunt, my mother's younger sister. She's not an Ashcroft and has nothing to do with this."

"Jillian *Ashcroft?*" Laura shouted.

Jill expected the roof to fall down over their heads, but nothing happened. Everyone remained frozen in their places, all eyes directed at her. She noticed the compassion mixed with frustration in Sir Richard's eyes, and from him she took the strength to go on.

"I lied to you, Laura, and I'm very, very sorry."

Laura's mouth pinched into a thin line, and Jill wondered if she would stalk out of the room and not let any explanation clear the air. Thank God she remained seated, however stiffly.

Jill launched into the story of her father's research and how he'd discovered the curse. "I intuitively know he's right, and I know the pendant will release the curse, but Cousin Alvin has put a spoke in the wheel today for the execution of my mission."

"You just planned to take it at your earliest convenience and not tell me?" Laura looked aghast.

"You never indicated that you wanted to part with it, Laura. I tried everything, and if I'd managed to take the pendant, I would have made an effort to clarify things with you. But I highly doubt that you would've let me speak my piece, and I doubt that you'll ever speak to me after today."

Laura had paled even more and rose to pace the room. Jill watched her, feeling as if only moments remained before the guillotine would fall.

"I know the Ashcrofts nearly destroyed our family. My father said that I should protect myself by wearing the pendant at all times."

"The Ashcrofts of old don't exist anymore," Jill said desperately.

Laura stood over her with the look of an avenging angel. "I'd say they do! See what you've done, wormed your way into the Keep under the pretext of being my friend, only with the purpose of stealing my pendant."

Sir Richard stepped forward. "Just to be fair, Jillian could never have gained access to this house had it not been for me. I agreed to help her in her mission, which I've bitterly regretted, but that doesn't remove any of my guilt." He bowed. "I'm deeply sorry to have hurt you in any way."

"You too?" Laura sank down on a sofa by the fireplace and put her head into her hands. "I'm completely at sea," she said to no one in particular.

Aunt Penelope sat down next to Laura and placed her arm around the younger woman. "There . . . there, my sweet." She gave Sir Richard a stare that would've withered a weaker man. As it was, he looked uncomfortable but determined.

Aunt Iddy sat down on another chair and fanned herself. "I've never been more mortified," she mumbled.

Laura cried softly into her hands, and Jill sat awash in guilt. She exchanged an uneasy glance with Sir

Richard, grateful that he'd taken part of the responsibility.

He cleared his throat and spoke, "Strangely enough, I believe Jill's story about her father and the curse. Her greatest crime in this was secrecy, but her reason for wanting the pendant is clear. She only wants to save her family, to be able to carry the Ashcroft name into the future. However, I told her on several occasions that she should've asked you for the pendant, Laura, and made a clean breast of things."

Laura wiped her red eyes and looked at Jill. "She knew I would never part with it. I found it strange that so many people developed an interest in it. No one ever took any notice before." She glanced toward the door. "I wonder what your cousin is planning."

A knock sounded and Brumley stepped inside. "You wanted me?" he asked Laura with a bow.

"Was there a gentleman here this morning?" she asked.

The butler nodded. "The young man who has been staying at Sandhurst, Mr. Alvin Ashcroft. He said he forgot some book or other the night he and the other gentlemen came for dinner. I let him in, thinking he would retrieve the book and leave. He went to the library and I took farewell of him about half an hour ago."

"He was here for about an hour?" Jill asked.

The butler nodded. "I let him out myself, and he carried a slim volume bound in leather. I assume you know about the matter."

No one replied and Brumley looked somewhat uncomfortable. He coughed discreetly. "Is there anything else?"

"No . . . ," Laura said, and the butler left. "Mr.

Ashcroft could've taken the pendant during that time period."

"I'm certain he did," Jill said. "No one else has any reason to take it. For most people it would appear worthless. After all, it's not a large diamond or a ruby."

She walked over to Laura and sank down on her knees. "I know what I'll do to repair this. I've realized this morning that your friendship means more to me than the pendant. It won't be difficult to locate my cousin, and when I do, you shall have your pendant back."

Silence hung in the room and Jill waited breathlessly for Laura's reply.

Her friend—until this morning—stared at her thoughtfully, but didn't speak.

"I'll return the pendant and pack my bags and leave posthaste. By tonight, this shall be nothing but a bad memory for you."

"Except that I shall have to nurse a great disappointment." She looked at Sir Richard. "And broken trust."

"Yes . . . I regret that this happened," Jill said. "I pray you can find forgiveness for your fiancé. In Sir Richard's favor I have to say that he greatly resisted my request of help. In fact, I had to blackmail him into it."

Aunt Iddy groaned as if in great pain and Jill wanted to do the same thing.

"I contrived this plan all by myself according to my father's findings. The curse should've been dispelled a long time ago, but none of my ancestors did anything about it, and I vowed I would, as I don't want to die young in some accident. I want to grow old and have grandchildren at my knee."

She placed a hand on Laura's arm for a moment.

"Believe me please, I never wanted to hurt *you*." She stood, her legs wobbly. "My greatest wish is that I could still call you my friend, but I realize I can't, so I'll go upon my mission to return the pendant. I hope you don't mind that my aunt stays here until I come back later this morning."

She didn't expect a reply from Laura. Giving Sir Richard what she hoped was a grateful smile, she left the room and closed the door quickly. Tears stung her eyes, but she pushed them away. She had to get hold of her rotten cousin before it was too late to repair the damage of her deception.

Fifteen

Later that morning, Sir Richard faced Laura in one of the parlors downstairs. Relieved that the truth had been revealed, he waited for his fiancée to speak.

Part of him longed for Jill whom he might never see again, and part of him wanted to do the honorable thing with Laura, especially after what happened this morning. In his heart, he realized he'd fallen in love with Jill, but that fact would have to be ignored. In time, he would forget her.

"I'm deeply disturbed over what happened," Laura said. "However, before I forgive you, I need to ask you a question."

"Yes, I'll answer anything you want to know honestly."

Laura stood, her back straight, her face pale but determined. "I understand Jill's claim that you had to give in to her demands for help."

"Yes."

"Did Jill truly blackmail you?"

He nodded, hesitant to speak of his past, but she needed to know the truth. "Jill knew about something that happened to my sister. All you know is that she passed away. We struggled in the family to keep everything a secret, and mostly succeeded, but Jill found out by a strange coincident. She used the knowledge because she needed my help with her mission."

He told Laura briefly about his sister's transgressions

and subsequent demise, and it pained him. It hurt to talk about the shame, but also to bring back the searing memory of her death. When he finished, he felt a strange sense of relief as if talking about Letitia eased his pain.

"I'm still reconciling myself to the fact that she's gone, and it's a struggle," he concluded. "Her life was cut off too early due to circumstances that could've been prevented."

Laura went to him and took his hands into hers. "I had no idea that you suffered such pain. Jill threatened to tell the world, didn't she?"

He nodded miserably. "But I have to confess that when I pressed the matter, and the only reason I agreed to aid her, was when she promised to remove her threat. She's never brought it up since, so I knew she was sincere." He studied Laura's earnest face. "I doubt that Jill desired to hurt you at all, not even before she met you. All she wanted was the pendant. She has no animosity toward the Endicott family, and I know she liked you the moment she set eyes on you."

"Just as I liked her," Laura replied with a grimace. "She still deceived me."

"Yes, that she did. She was adamant about keeping the whole thing a secret because she knew you would not part with the pendant. I doubt that she thrived on the idea that she had to steal it from you. I know she agonized over it."

"I *knew* there was something odd about her appearance here. You seemed to be at loggerheads most of the time, not great friends."

"I was violently opposed to the scheme from the moment I heard of it, and I let her know that in no uncertain terms."

Laura looked deeply into his eyes, and possibly

wanted him to take her into his arms, but he couldn't move. She finally pulled her hands from his, and went to stand by the window.

"This issue is separate from what is evolving between us, Richard. I understand your involvement in Jill's scheme, and I'm no longer angry with you for that. You were a pawn in her game." She took a deep breath. "However, I'm disappointed that you won't stand up and admit that you have no deeper feelings for me than friendship."

"A pledge is a pledge," he replied defensively.

"I'll have you know I don't intend to enter a loveless marriage," she said, her voice rising. "I'm appalled that you would be willing to do that, and it shows me that you don't listen to the voice in your heart."

He hung his head. "You're right, I suppose. I've never been accustomed to . . . ahem, listen. I don't know about that voice."

"It's about time that you do. I know in my heart that you don't love me, and the truth is that I don't have a *tendre* for you, either. We would be ill-advised to do anything together except remain friends."

"You'd be willing to remain my friend after everything that has happened?" He looked at her incredulously. Laura had a very large heart, a glimpse of which he saw more every day. "Maybe in time we could find a deeper connection."

"Please," she said. "When you kissed me, it felt as if I'd been kissed by a brother."

"That is a rather cruel thing to say."

"But true nevertheless, and truth is what we need more of around here. We've been sadly lacking in that area, but never again."

He heaved a deep sigh. For some reason he couldn't explain, a huge burden lifted from his shoulders. He'd been so blind, but also so stuck in the stuffy idea that duty came before love.

Love. He did know love. It had just recently been awakened in his heart, and he would have to find the courage to pursue it.

"Have you found love then?" he finally asked Laura.

She smiled, a film of tears veiling her eyes. He saw her magnificence, her courage. Other women might swoon at such setbacks as Laura had endured this morning, but she rose to every challenge without cringing.

"Perhaps."

"It must be Julian because I haven't seen you as animated with any other gentleman."

She nodded. "Yes . . . I believe I'm in love with Julian. He makes my heart make peculiar somersaults in my chest."

"I know that feeling," he said simply.

"Jill ignited that passion in you, didn't she?" she proclaimed without ado. "You must go to her and tell her."

"I am torn in my loyalty, which has nothing to do with my feelings. She betrayed you, and I don't want to see you suffer from that. I do believe she will return the pendant if it's in her power."

Laura sighed, drying her eyes on a handkerchief. "Basically she's a good person, only misguided."

He nodded. "Well, yes, her beliefs are rather unorthodox. What about you? Can you accept the claim that the Endicotts placed a curse upon the Ashcrofts?"

"Yes, that's a possibility, but it's not part of recent family history. There are no metaphysicians in my family—as far as I know. We are a somewhat dull lot."

He smiled. "I do recall someone who maintains that animals talk to her."

Laura returned his smile. "There's that. It's such a part of my life I never think about it. Sometimes I know what people are thinking, or what they are going to say before they say it, but I've never made much of it."

"I'd say those are talents that frighten most people."

"But not you, Richard?"

He shook his head. "I don't know what to believe, but I try to keep an open mind."

"Which is a strike in your favor." Laura went across the room to his side and took one of his hands. "I want you to be happy, and I always appreciated your willingness to care for me and mine. But you have to find your own happiness, and I pray we'll always be friends."

"You have my word on that," he said and kissed her hand. "Thank you for your readiness to forgive me."

She inclined her head in acknowledgment. "I believe it's necessary that we follow Jill."

He stared at her incredulously. "You do? I thought you'd never want to see her again."

"I need to talk with her more about the past."

"You're not angry with her?"

"Yes, I am, but I'm willing to overlook my feelings to get some answers."

He nodded, too surprised to reply.

A knock sounded on the door and Brumley announced Julian's arrival. The viscount stepped inside, and Laura ran to his side. With a wide smile, he kissed her on the cheek. He gave Sir Richard a searching stare as if to gauge his reaction to Laura's friendliness.

Sir Richard greeted him pleasantly, still unable to make up his mind whether he liked the man or not. Even though Julian always acted amicably and with great charm that appealed to the ladies, something appeared hidden, simmering right under the surface.

"Julian, I would like you to accompany Richard and me on a mission."

Sir Richard gave her a narrow stare as he realized that she firmly believed he would go after Jill. He had no choice, and her gaze said as much.

"And then escort me back home if Richard has to return to Eversley after the mission has been accomplished," she continued.

Julian executed a small bow. "It shall be my pleasure. Can I ask where we're going?"

"We might travel all the way to Devon, depending on the circumstances," Sir Richard answered for Laura. "But we might catch up with Jillian sooner."

"Jillian?"

Laura gave him a brief explanation. "Jill may need our help as her cousin is not a gentleman to be trusted."

"She's Alvin's cousin?"

"It's a long story, Julian. I'll tell you the whole when we're on our way," Laura said. "I'm going to don my riding habit and call for the horses to be saddled."

When Laura had left the room, the two men faced each other. Sir Richard decided to confront Julian with the truth.

"I hear you have developed a *tendre* for the fair Laura, and she for you."

Julian had the decency to look uncomfortable. "Yes . . . she's a precious pearl. My increasing feelings for her grew most uncomfortable as the date for your nuptials came closer."

"As long as your feelings are sincere I have nothing to complain about, but if you're only interested in her for her adjoining land, I shall personally pierce you through the heart with steel."

A flash of temper burned in Julian's eyes. "I have nothing but honorable intentions toward her."

"I still feel responsible for Laura, and I'll make sure she's happy, even if I'm not the man for her."

Julian did not reply; color had risen in his cheeks, and Sir Richard noticed that he kept his temper firmly in check even as it boiled hot beneath the surface.

Sir Richard walked toward the door. "See you at the stables."

He waited for Laura to come downstairs, and when she did, he pulled her aside as she donned her tight riding gloves. "I need to say something about Julian," he said. "If you're truly happy, I have nothing to admonish you about, but if you have the slightest hesitation about his feelings, or his intention, you have to tell me. And you have to be honest with yourself. Are you sure he'll make you happy?"

She got a faraway look in her eyes. "I . . . don't . . . know, Richard."

"Just don't let him push you into anything, or any decision that doesn't feel right to you. From now on, he has to answer to me. I won't let him turn your head completely, unless you're completely sure he's the man you want."

She smiled and placed her hand on his arm. Her face looked almost transparent, and dark smudges of fatigue colored the delicate skin under her eyes. "Thank you. I will let you know when I've made up my mind if Julian is the man for me. Meanwhile, I'm happy. He's brought romance to my life, and it's a whole new chapter."

Sir Richard laughed gruffly. "That it is. You and I have brought new chapters into our lives, but only the Almighty knows what's written there."

She nodded. "Yes, but I'd like to explore."

"Let's go then; let's clear up the old."

Jill rode hard to catch up with her cousin. One of the grooms had accompanied her as protection, and she was grateful for his company as she strived to find Alvin. She knew her cousin would await her at Lindenwood if she couldn't catch up with him sooner. She had every intention of finding him at the next inn along the road. In the distance she could see the moor stretching endlessly. The hamlets and villages along her route were few and far between.

Sorrow and regret filled her heart at this morning's revelations. She wished she could start this mission over, this time for the best of everyone. As she'd hurt Laura's feelings, she'd hurt her own.

"Dratted stupidity," she mumbled to herself, fighting the urge to cry. She gritted her teeth and forged on. When she found Alvin, she would, if not kill him, maim him, she thought. Slowly.

Hedges lined the road and finches flew in mad dashes from tree to tree as they sang to each other. The lane emerged into a village by the name of Tregaron Pond. Thatched roofs covered most of the stone cottages, and she looked for the sign that would identify the inn or hostelry. The Ale Barrel came into view around a bend in the lane.

The cross-timbered building brooded at the edge of the village green, its small windows closed to the world. Sparrows pecked in the dirt outside the door.

Jill's mount scattered a gaggle of geese that squawked with annoyance. She pulled to a halt outside the roughly timbered door of the inn. The gaily painted sign flapped in the wind, and dust made swirls along the ground. The groom took the reins of her horse as she went inside. As she'd predicted, she'd found Alvin.

He sat at one of the tables drinking a tankard of ale and chewing on bread and a slab of ham liberally slathered with mustard. He stopped in the middle of a bite and stared at her. Setting down his food, he said, "I suspected you would come haring after me."

"Of all the hen-witted things to do!" she snapped, standing over him, her fists clenched. "Why did you steal the pendant?"

"When I understood how important it was to you, I collected it. It belongs to us, don't you think?"

"Have you completely lost your marbles?" A seething, boiling fury overcame her, and she struggled to prevent falling into a bout of fisticuffs with him.

"I only need the pendant to put an end to the family curse. I don't pretend it belongs to us; it's not a matter of family pride as you seem to think." She held out her hand toward him. "Give me the pendant now."

He laughed. "You must be about in your head, Coz. The pendant is my trump card. If I'm to hand it over, I expect something in return."

"That's ludicrous. Why would you want to ruin my plans—plans of which I made you aware."

"Yes, I can see your point, but you're so unreasonable that I have to make you see mine. I'm tired of your rejection."

"Fustian!"

He set down the tankard with a thud. "If you want to see the pendant ever again, you'll have to marry me."

"You imbecile! The curse has to be lifted during the next full moon. That's tomorrow night."

"We can procure a special license. I have contacts in London. There are no more excuses. We were meant to be together, and I'll make sure that it'll happen as I see fit. This time you'll have to do as I say. You can't fight me forever, not as long as I have the pendant."

"You're a conniver of the worst kind. If you don't give me the pendant now, I shall personally see to it that the curse touches you with vengeance. I confided in you about everything and you repay me with deceit and extortion."

"Be that as it may. The only way I can see success in my future is to have my hand on your purse strings."

Jill snorted in a most unladylike fashion. "At least you're honest, but I'll have you know that I'd rather be dead than have to marry you."

"If you were, I would inherit your money," he said nastily.

"No, you wouldn't. My mother's inheritance is free of any encumbrances, so it won't go to you. I have written a will making the nunnery in Plymouth the sole beneficiary."

His jaw dropped. "You cannot be that cruel, Coz."

"Yes, I can, if only to save my own hide from your murderous intent. I saw your true colors a long time ago, and I know both our fathers would turn in their graves at your disgrace." She stepped close and bent over him so that only inches separated their noses.

"Now, give me the pendant."

He shook his head mutely.

"If you don't give it to me, I shall—"

"What will you do?" he chided. "Plant me a facer? I doubt that very much." He gave a nervous laugh and wiped his hands down the front of his coat as if readying himself for a fight. It wouldn't be the first one they'd had.

She would do just that, but two farmers stepped into the taproom, eyeing her with curiosity. A lady did not enter a fight unless she yearned to cause a scandal. It may be much more favorable to steal the pendant from Alvin at night as he usually retired three sheets to the wind from drinking brandy all evening. She doubted his habits had changed.

"I'll talk with you shortly," she said and marched out of the room. The sunlight blinded her outside and the groom from the Keep eyed her speculatively.

"Are we going back now?" he asked, surely wanting to get back to familiar grounds.

"Not yet, Rupert." She handed him coins from her purse. "Find some victuals for me and yourself, and slake your thirst. I hear the ale inside is very good."

He took the money and she wished she could ask him to knock Alvin to the ground to give her a chance to find the pendant, but she needed to think and plan her strategy before she asked for Rupert's help. He might not be easy to convince.

Laura, Sir Richard, and Julian rode along the path that Jill had taken some hours earlier. They came to Tregannon Pond and asked at the local inn if anyone by Jill's description had passed through. The innkeeper gave them the information that she had arrived hot on the heels of a young gentleman. They had heated words, ate a hot meal and drank some ale, then left together, one groom in tow.

"Left together?" Laura said. "She hated Alvin as far as I know."

"Perhaps it was all a sham, just part of the whole plan," Julian suggested.

The only one who didn't want to believe that was

Sir Richard. Surely Jill's disgust for her cousin had been real? But maybe they had believed what she'd wanted them to believe.

He didn't know what was true anymore. "Let's keep our judgment private until we have a chance to confront Jill," he said.

"Yes . . . you're right, Richard," Laura said. She gave him a long look, evidently seeing his discomfort.

Julian leaned across from his saddle to squeeze Laura's hand. "We shall get through this, my sweet."

Laura smiled valiantly. "Yes, I know we will."

"By nightfall, the pendant shall hang around your neck anew," he continued. "I shall personally see to it."

That however, was too optimistic a prediction. They had to ride all the way to Lindenwood, a journey lasting a day and a half, to catch up with Jill and Alvin. By then, they were all exhausted, especially Laura.

Sixteen

Jill drew in a deep breath of pleasure to be at her ancestral home again. The estate had derived its name from the many lindens that grew on the property, and they seemed to wave a welcome in the stiff breeze. Jill had missed them as they had sheltered her many times over the years. She remembered climbing the great majority of them in her childhood.

She had barely spoken with Alvin during their seemingly endless journey, and her plan to retrieve the pendant from him had not worked as she discovered that first night that he wore it around his neck.

That arrangement ought to make him particularly accident prone, she thought, but nothing had happened to him. A pity, really.

Nothing ever seemed to happen to him.

The rolling parkland and the majestic curving drive invited her, and the familiar vista of the house made her heart squeeze with longing for her father. His very footsteps still seemed to echo on the flagstones between the main house and the building where he'd had his laboratory. Herbs still lined every shelf as they had during his lifetime.

The old Elizabethan-style mansion basked in the golden afternoon sunlight, ivy climbing over the two wings flanking the main part. The windowpanes winked reflections from the sun, and flowering bushes softened the majestic walls. Despite its size, the estate always looked welcoming to her.

It sat like an elegant jewel in the peaceful and lush setting of the parkland that surrounded it. Where the Keep had been stark and forbidding, Lindenwood always welcomed one.

"Home at last," Alvin said after riding in sullen silence for most of the day. "I'm certain you'll agree with me that this is *home*. You can deny it all you want, but I know how you feel about Lindenwood." He snorted a laugh. "You can't stay away from here."

Jill grimaced. She would never allow him to be right. If it weren't for imbecile laws that females could not inherit entailed property, she would live here.

"You've got windmills in your head if you believe I will live here," she replied. "With you. I'd rather be drawn and quartered before that ever happens."

"You'll have to set your cap for some half-witted gentleman just to find a permanent roof over your head. No one else will have you."

"Are you implying that I'm so totty-headed I can't find a normal gentleman?" she asked coldly. "I daresay you're totally wrong."

"Needle-witted you ain't," he said with another snort.

Anger seethed in her chest. "There's no use wasting my energy on you, Alvin. *You* are the yokel here. As I said, I'd rather be drawn and quartered before living with you—anywhere and for any length of time."

They rode to the front door in stiff animosity, and she sensed that Alvin strained mentally to come up with something that would change her mind.

She would've felt some pity for him if it hadn't been for his malicious bent. He was cold-hearted and calculating, and she suspected that most people found that out rather quickly. It would be hard for him to find some unsuspecting female to marry him. She would have to be somewhat naïve to fall for his self-serving charm.

Without a word, he handed over the reins to the approaching groom, and then walked into the mansion without a backward glance at her. She followed, and old Mr. Biggins, the butler, greeted her warmly.

"Miss, it warms my heart to see you here at Lindenwood. We have all missed you."

Jill smiled. "I've missed you too, but this is no longer my home, and we have to make do."

Biggins gave a resigned smile. "Aye, miss, we go on, day after day, year after year. And your aunt, how is she, if I may ask?"

"She's in good vigor, Biggins."

Jill went through the familiar rooms, the furniture now shrouded in holland covers. The house held an air of abandonment, and that only reminded her that she had nothing here, only memories that would never come alive again. She had to let go of this place.

Going to the window in the back parlor, she looked out over the parkland. In the distance she could glimpse the glittering water of the Channel. She had to head down to the shore tonight, during the full moon.

Closing her eyes and sighing, she wondered why she had to face so much struggle, and why obtaining the pendant still eluded her. She would not go to the sea empty-handed tonight even if she bodily had to fight Alvin to get the pendant.

"I'll even help you with the ceremony tonight in return for your promise of wedded bliss," Alvin said behind her as he entered the room.

"Don't be silly, Alvin." All she had to do was promise,

but promises could be broken, couldn't they? Perhaps she should play along and see if she had better success accomplishing her mission. Everything in her rebelled against that kind of manipulation.

"It's your choice. After tonight, your mission will be lost, Coz."

"Yes . . . perhaps I was meant to fail." She swept out her arm. "Don't you care about anything? Don't you have any feelings for this magnificent estate? If you did, you would hurry to aid me to accomplish what I set out to do." With one contemptuous glance, she marched past him.

Somehow she felt suffocated in the house with him. Walking back outside, she headed toward the stables. She needed to think, and decided to ride down to the sea. Maybe the water and the beautiful ancient oak that grew in lone majesty where the park ended and the rocky shore began would give her some insight that she badly needed.

She sat on a rock ledge halfway down the steep descent to the shore. The sea sent long, lazy waves crashing among the rocks below, and she pondered the strength and power of that water.

Everything had its own unhurried rhythm. Why was it that she felt so separated from that rhythm? Her life consisted of struggle and disappointments. Ever since she found out about the curse, she'd worked toward dissolving it with single-minded determination. There had been no time for any other kind of life.

As she leaned back against the hollow of a rotten tree root embedded in the rocks, she let her thoughts drift to Sir Richard. She fought not to think of him, but his face came unbidden into her mind.

Her longing sat hollow in her chest, and she feared

he would never speak to her again, not after what had happened at the Keep.

"Drat it all," she said to herself. "Why did I ever have to clap eyes on him? My life is more complicated than ever, thanks to him. I never counted on returning to Lindenwood heartbroken."

She closed her eyes and struggled to think of something else, but the memory of their kisses came to her before she could force them out of her mind. Somewhere during her stay at the Keep she had fallen deeply in love with him. He was something else that had become unattainable.

"Nothing but cursed nuisance," she muttered as her eyes grew heavier with every beat of the waves against the rocks. Pain lodged in her throat from unshed tears.

"You have to forget that he ever existed," she told herself, tears now burning on the insides of her eyelids.

Her thoughts roving aimlessly, they created havoc with her emotions, and she wished she could find a way to take the next step. Everything she'd planned for had gone awry, and she could see no solution to her dilemma.

Her heart leaden, she nodded off, exhaustion claiming her body. She had no idea how long she slept, but when she awakened, the sun had just set in the West, leaving scarves of orange and yellow wafting across the silver blue sky. The beauty of the sunset took her breath away.

Her legs stiff, she forced herself to an upright position and stretched. The catnap had strengthened her, and a spurt of determination ran through her. She would have another try at gaining the Endicott pendant. With any luck, Alvin would be so drunk that he wouldn't notice if she tore it off his throat.

If all else failed, she would threaten him with one of his pistols. She would have one of the grooms load it for her.

She didn't want to resort to such threats, she thought with a deep sigh.

Her body stiff from her reclining position, she walked up the path to the top. The view halted her progress as she watched the last of the orange fade away. She'd tied her horse to the ancient tree that stood in lonely stateliness at the edge of the property.

A few birds still twittered among the branches, but they would fall silent as darkness crept across the sky. She touched the rough bark of the oak, sensing the strength and hardiness of the tree.

It had always protected Lindenwood, and it always would, she thought, something akin to longing in her chest squeezing tight. "Oh, Father," she whispered, "I wish you were with me tonight. I dearly need your advice."

Nothing came to her and she felt ready to cry, but bit back her tears. This was not the time to become emotional. She stared for a long time out to sea as darkness fell like a soft mantle around her. The stars twinkled to life across the sky, one after the other, and she counted them aimlessly until the moon began its voyage across the firmament. Huge and silver, it hung in its lonely, indifferent glory.

She sat against the tree trunk, waiting, but she did not know for what. The silver disk transfixed her. Unseen powers must hold this world as the moon moved around it, but if someone asked her about the mystery of the silver planet's pull, Jill would not be able to explain it.

There was magic, always would be.

She had no idea how long she'd been sitting

against the tree. Her back prickled and her legs had lost all feeling as she tried to move them. The blood flooding through sent tiny needles down her legs.

She got up, her body uncomfortable. It was time to do something. She couldn't just let this night slip away without some results.

Grimly set on facing Alvin yet again, she went to her horse that kept nibbling the grass at the base of the tree. As she released the reins, she heard hoofbeats along the path, and fear ran through her for a moment. What was he up to now?

"Coz? Is that you?" came Alvin's voice in the dark.

"Yes," she replied. He had come to her. Good, this saved her from having to confront him in the house. "I hope you brought the pendant. The moon is full, and I have the ingredients for the ceremony in my saddlebags."

He didn't reply, and she sensed he would not give her any kind of support, the dratted popinjay.

"It's for your own good, Alvin."

"Be that as it may. I won't give in until you promise to marry me."

"I'll pay your debts. You can start afresh," she countered.

"Be my wife."

"So that you can squander my inheritance at the gaming tables? Never. That would be like giving myself a death sentence."

"Who said anything about squandering? I'm not a complete flat."

Yes, you are, she thought. "I cannot marry you."

He got off his horse and came to stand over her. Inwardly, she cringed, but outwardly she held her stance. Despite his lack of height, he appeared threatening in the darkness, his black cloak fluttering in the breeze off the water. He certainly had the Ashcroft stubbornness, a curse in itself.

"You have no choice but to marry me if you want to succeed with your plans," he said, an edge of menace in his voice.

She stiffened, the hairs at the back of her neck rising. "Are you threatening me?"

He didn't reply, only gripped her arms and began to pull her toward him. Just the thought of having to endure his embrace made her feel sick. She pushed against him.

"Enough is enough, Alvin. Desist!"

He held her even tighter, and anger blossomed hot and hard in her chest. With a mighty shove, she released his hold and managed to get away. "Don't touch me again."

She saw against the sky that he was shaking his head. As he reached out to grip her again, she swung a fist at his face. It connected against bone, sending spears of pain through her hand.

"Aoow," he growled, clutching his jaw.

She swung at him again, this time aiming for his stomach. He doubled over, and she realized her swing had more power than she thought.

As he staggered forward, she chopped both fists against his neck, and he fell. She got down beside him and searched frantically for the pendant. It dangled on its chain around his neck, but as she tried to wiggle it free, he grappled with her.

Going down in a heap of flailing arms and legs, they fought furiously.

Jill had never been more determined to succeed. She clawed and kicked, punched, kneed, and elbowed, but he remained stronger, now that he knew what to expect from her.

She lost her breath in the melee, and found herself no closer to retrieving the pendant.

He finally shook her off, rose on unsteady legs, and with a show of defiance in the silver moonlight, tore the pendant from his neck, chain dangling, and hurled it into the black and restless ocean below.

"No!" Jill screamed with anger and frustration. "How could you?"

"Watch me, you thimblewit." He sounded so angry she thought he would attack her once again.

She ached all over and fell onto her back, as the scenario of her failure went through her head. *Too late!* she screamed in her head, *too late . . .*

Moaning, she rose to her knees, and before she knew it, he had hauled her into his arms and tried to kiss her.

She slammed a knee into his crotch, and he partly let go of her as he groaned with pain, but she couldn't quite wiggle free.

Tears of rage and frustration flooded her eyes. "This is the outside of enough." She kicked his leg hard, which only enraged him more.

Exhausted, she fought him with aching fists, but feared she'd entered a losing battle as his superior strength came into play once again.

She heard the sounds of horses vaguely, but she struggled too hard to get off the ground to really pay any attention. Only when the menace of Alvin was lifted from her by the force of outside powers did she realize that they were no longer alone.

She heard Alvin groaning as someone knocked him down with one massive blow.

Panting, she lay in the grass, staring up at the sky. She heard male and female voices, and she wondered who had come to rescue her. When she regained her breath, she sat up, her head swimming.

"Who—?"

"Jill?"

She recognized Sir Richard's voice.

"You! What are you doing here, Sir Richard?"

He didn't reply as he bent down to check if Alvin still had any fight left in him.

"Jill?" she heard a female call out.

"Laura?" A sinking feeling went through Jill. Would she have to face a confrontation with the woman she'd grown to call her friend?

"Jill, I'm not here to argue and demand restitution."

Relieved beyond words, Jill scrambled to her feet. "Thank you," she said, still feeling faint from her fight with Alvin. "He threw the pendant into the sea."

"I see." Laura evidently knew immediately. "Your mission has been foiled then."

Jill wiped her face where tears had begun to fall. "Yes. Of all bacon-brained things, Alvin has never understood the danger he's in."

"You truly believe in the curse?" Laura asked. Her mount stood next to Jill, who struggled to stay upright. She leaned against the horse's warm and velvet-soft neck and fought back her anger and sorrow.

"Yes, I do."

Laura slid out of the saddle and stood beside her.

Jill sobbed, feeling exposed even if the night held sway, lit only with silvery moonlight. She longed to throw her arms around Laura and ask for her forgiveness, but she couldn't move. She couldn't hide her distress and it bothered her.

When Laura touched her arm, she flinched.

"Don't worry. I'm not angry with you anymore, Jill."

Jill couldn't believe her ears, and she stared with aching eyes at her friend.

"I understand why you acted the way you did," Laura continued. "You thought of the Endicotts as your enemy, as they always have been—even if the animosity of the past has been long forgotten."

"I hoped stupidly enough at one point that you would give me the pendant, which would have made things much easier." Jill drew a deep shuddering breath. "I can't tell you how sorry I am."

"And you didn't know me. I could've been as evil as that ancient Lucinda who began all this nonsense."

"Once I had entered the deception, I could not pull back out." Jill leaned against the horse's warm flank. "And now it's too late. My silly cousin made sure of that. I don't know how to repay you for the lost pendant."

Laura stood silent as if pondering something.

"Believe me, if I could start over from the moment I walked into the Keep that first time, I would. I saw right away that you were no evil witch."

"All you needed for breaking the curse was the pendant?" Laura asked.

"Yes, I have herbs that drive out the spell and magic that my father discovered during his course of study. Timing is of the essence." She glanced at the moon, then at Alvin who was now sitting up, rubbing his chin. An urge to pummel him came over her again, but it would be pointless.

"Too late now," she said, feeling the entire depth of her frustration.

Laura glanced at Alvin, then at Sir Richard who stood over the younger man. Julian still remained in the saddle, his attention pinned on Laura. Jill wondered why he had accompanied Laura and Sir Richard, and she sensed a change. Something had happened since she left the Keep.

Sir Richard ambled over to them. "I don't think Alvin will bother you again, Jill."

Jill sighed. "As long as he's alive, he'll bother me. I daresay I'm used to it."

She glanced at the moon that stood high and clear above them. The light reflected silver in Sir Richard's eyes. He looked at her very closely, and Jill wondered at his scrutiny, which made her heart pound. His presence had a strange effect on her. It must be the full moon.

He touched her cheek, which still held the wetness of tears. With one finger he gently wiped them off, a gesture that took her completely by surprise. For some reason he'd changed. Feeling guilty over his show of tenderness right in front of his fiancée, she looked from him to Laura, who didn't seem overly concerned.

Come to think of it, she looked almost pleased. And there was definitely inexplicable warmth in Sir Richard's eyes. When had that change come to pass?

"I don't know what to do now," she whispered to no one in particular. "My legs are shaking so badly I can barely stand, and Alvin has ruined my chances to set things right."

Laura held out her hand. "Speaking for our generation of Endicotts and Ashcrofts, I offer peace and friendship between the families, now and forever."

Jill's breath caught in her throat. She didn't feel worthy of such friendship as Laura offered, but she would rather die than turn it down. She took Laura's hand and pulled her close for a hug.

"Thank you, Laura," she whispered, once again overcome with emotion. She sniveled into Laura's shoulder. "You're the kindest person I've ever met. I just cannot thank you enough."

"Perhaps if you say it a million times. You're the most courageous person I've ever met," Laura said simply.

"Courageous? 'Twas rather lily-livered of me to deceive you."

"You had the gumption to overcome all obstacles." She reached into the pocket of her riding habit. "I rode all this way wondering if I'd ever extend this to you."

She pulled out her hand, which held a small leather pouch with a dangling drawstring. Opening it, she poured something into Jill's hand. A smooth roundness touched her aching skin, and the shape appeared familiar. She gazed at it in the moonlight. The pendant!

"How? Where?" she gasped, glancing out to sea where the other had disappeared.

"This is the real pendant. My grandfather had a replica made, which I've been wearing since everyone showed such interest in the pendant. I was afraid something would happen to it, and it did."

"Perhaps you sensed the threat," Sir Richard said.

Laura nodded. "I knew some skulduggery was underfoot, but nothing about the details. During my lifetime no one ever desired to acquire the pendant. Most people thought it wasn't good enough to wear."

Jill was acutely aware of the power of the rock. She compared it to holding a magnet to iron. It almost made her sick to her stomach and she longed to put it down, but that would be the last thing she'd do. Finally, through a miracle, her goal had become achievable.

"I wondered why Alvin could wear the pendant around his neck on the way here without having any kind of mishap. I even started doubting my own sanity," Jill said.

"He wore the replica, and threw that in the sea. Now there's only the real thing left," Laura said. She reached out and closed Jill's hand around the pendant. "It's yours now, and I know you aim to destroy it."

"Won't you miss it?"

Laura looked at Jill's closed hand. "Yes, possibly, but I have more than one family heirloom, and I want any feuds cleared up, especially now that I've found some new friends to brighten my life."

"The best spell breaker might be to make friends with the enemy," Sir Richard said with a laugh.

"Says the man who didn't believe in magic," Jill said caustically.

"With the kind of dedication you displayed the last few weeks, there must be some truth to the legend, or you're completely queer in the attic." Sir Richard stared at her, a smile playing on his lips in the moonlight. "I'll have to make up my mind about that."

Jill felt too subdued after all the turmoil to invent a witty reply. She gazed at the pendant in her hand, then at the moon that stood full and regal above them. "I believe it's time."

In silence they watched her open one of the saddlebags and pull out a small cloth bag tied at the top. She glanced from one to the other, and Julian had also joined the group. He stood close to Laura. It almost looked as if he were holding his arm around her. The light and the shadows played tricks on her eyes, surely?

Refusing to let her mind wander onto that subject, she led the way to the mighty oak some distance from the cliffs. Sir Richard had fallen into step beside her.

"Are we going to see spirits and smoke?"

"Where did you get that idea, Sir Richard?"

"Magic tricks are more often than not displayed

with a lot of smoke, with chilling disembodied voices moaning in the background."

"I doubt we'll see or hear anything out of the ordinary," Jill replied dryly. "And this is not a *trick.*"

He didn't reply to that.

Alvin came running after the group and Sir Richard commanded that he stay back, but Jill put her hand on his arm. "He might leave me alone from now on if he's part of the ceremony. Since he's an Ashcroft, he has the right to take part even if I highly dislike him."

Sir Richard grimaced, but she ignored him.

"What are you doing, Jill?" Alvin asked peevishly.

"I'm fulfilling the plan I had before you threw the pendant into the sea."

"How's that possible?" he asked as he cradled his swelling chin. He had difficulty keeping up with her rapid stride, and stumbled repeatedly on tufts of grass.

"Anything is possible when you have really good friends." Jill glanced over her shoulder at Laura and Julian who walked awfully close together, whispering things to each other. If she wasn't mistaken, those two were more than friends, but how could that be?

They arrived at the tree, and when Jill stood on the opposite side, she could clearly see the moon between the spokes of a Y formed in the branches. This was the magic spot. She'd read the instructions so many times she knew them by heart. Her father would be pleased tonight.

This was the year and the day that her sire had calculated. She prayed that his calculations were correct. All she could do was trust.

Laura came to stand beside her. "What do we do now?"

"You can all hold the prayer that all ill will and

wrongdoing perpetrated by the two families is now forever gone." Jill got down on her knees and dug a hole at the base of the trunk with her gloved hands. It didn't have to be deep, just really in the right area.

Standing where she could see in the light cast by the moon, she untied her cloth bag and studied the contents.

Gently placing the pendant on the ground, she sank to her knees and pulled out packets of dried powdered herbs and flowers. There was pine, peony, hydrangea, fumitory, and dragon's blood, and an incantation written on a piece of paper.

She sprinkled some herbs on the paper, and then tied it around the pendant with the chain. Under her breath, she repeated the invocation eleven times while tying string all around the pendant.

Per her father's instructions, she sprinkled powdered frankincense all around the hole she'd dug and over the pendant. More herbs followed, and finally she said a prayer for release and forgiveness.

Tears spilled down her cheeks as she buried the pendant in the hole, covered over it with dirt, and sprinkled the rest of the herbs all around it.

She waited, feeling the air around her. As she held her hands on the ground over the hole, a strange power seemed to rise through her hands like a wave, then seemingly dissolved.

Suddenly, a bird the size of a crow lifted from the branches of the tree, giving a guttural shriek. She hadn't noticed it before.

Then she heard nothing but the sound of the waves crashing in the sea. Everyone remained motionless and silent.

The bird circled in the air above, its black wings painted silver by the moon. Giving another harsh cry and rustling its feathers, it seemed to fly straight up into the sky.

"What was that?" Alvin asked in a frightened voice.

"Perhaps the spirit that had been trapped," Laura said, and it sounded right, but rather strange, Jill thought.

Everyone seemed to ponder that statement and no one wanted to make a comment. The air was hushed as if waiting for something, but that sensation passed as a flock of birds darted on silent wings through the night.

The sound of the waves increased to Jill's acute hearing, but it might just be her imagination playing tricks. Something had changed and the restlessness that had been hounding her appeared to be gone.

Instead, her heart was filled with peace, and at this very moment, she didn't care what happened in the future, and she didn't care that her body ached relentlessly.

She glanced at Laura, who also looked peaceful. Laura smiled, and Jill noticed that she was holding Julian's hand. Someone would have to explain this new startling development to her. Perhaps it wasn't startling at all.

"Thank you for your assistance," she said to everyone. "I know this whole chapter appears most peculiar, but I know something came to a close tonight. I trust that I'll never have to find another spell remover or herbal treatment. The Ashcrofts are safe, thanks to you, Laura."

She went to take Laura's other hand. "You gave me a great gift tonight, and I'm forever beholden to you."

"It may seem strange, but I feel as if a burden has been lifted from me, and I'm actually glad that the pendant is gone. I believe the spell held me trapped as well.

Despite everything that has happened, I'm glad it happened the way it did. It worked out perfectly."

Jill nodded. "That it did."

Sir Richard pulled her by the elbow. "I need to speak with you," he said.

"I hope you won't scold me for the ceremony that I performed," she replied, apprehensive now that it was all over. She did care what Sir Richard thought about her. Her legs dragged as he pulled her along.

"No, I won't scold you. Not now, not ever, not for something you truly believe in. If we don't have convictions, where does our purpose go?"

They walked through the grass past Alvin sitting on the ground. He sat very still, head in his hands as if dejected or in deep pain.

Evidently he'd given up any attempt at getting his own way, and Jill drew a sigh of relief. Sir Richard pulled her quickly past him as if urging her not to address her cousin.

"I need to talk with you most urgently," he whispered. "I've been most anxious to address this matter."

Jill didn't think she'd ever seen him that animated. His smile flashed in the moonlight, and he wrapped his arm around her.

They stood together among some rocks, staring at the dark, restless sea. Then he took her by the shoulders and turned her around, until she faced him. Her heartbeat escalated and she wondered what he had on his mind. Whatever it was, she knew he wasn't about to berate her for the past.

In fact, everything had turned out beautifully, and she still had a wonderful friend in Laura.

"I'm so grateful," she said. "I know I've said it before, but it can't be repeated enough."

"By Jupiter, you sound as if you've been blessed by the Holy Mother herself."

"In a sense, I have. Some kind of unseen force took pity on me and helped me to accomplish my goal."

"There's only one missing piece."

She could barely breathe by now as she felt the full strength of his attention directed at her. His arm comforted and cradled her. "What piece?"

"This moment. There's so much I've been longing to say to you since we left the Keep. This trip has truly been a lesson in patience."

"I've noticed that you and Laura no longer seem to be engaged."

"That's correct. She has a *tendre* for Julian, and obviously he has one for her. At least I hope he does because she has starlight in her eyes every time she looks at him. I wish her to be happy."

Jill nodded. "I noticed that starlight as well."

"She gave me her congé two days ago, but we'll remain friends as I have no desire to put her out of my life. Her rejection made me happy, gave me new hope."

"That's rare from those who were betrothed only days ago, and planning the actual nuptial ceremony."

"You're right. Aren't you going to say that I'm a regular cod's head or something?"

"No, Sir Richard, I have no intention of sparring with you over something that doesn't even concern me."

"But it does," he said and put his arms around her waist and pulled her very close. "If Laura and I hadn't broken off, we—you and I—would not have this chance."

"Sir Richard—"

"It's Richard," he said, "and I suggest that you say

'yes, Richard' to my proposal." He pulled her so tight she felt faint for a moment. "I love you, Jillian Ashcroft. Do you want to become my wife just as fast as we can procure a special license? As in tomorrow?"

Even though she'd suspected he would propose to her, it still came as a surprise. "When did you realize you were in love with me?"

"That day when I kissed you on the lookout at the Keep. Something wonderful ignited inside of me." He touched her lips lightly with his. "I'm madly, irrevocably in love with you, Jill. You challenged my regimented life—opened me up to possibilities. I was always drawn to your boundless enthusiasm. You never let setbacks hamper you."

"If you do, no great goal can be accomplished," she whispered, acutely aware of the scent of his skin and the feel of his strong shoulders under her hands.

"Please, Jill, release mè from the terror of not knowing. Will you become my wife?"

She wanted to faint with bliss, but she managed a small croak. "Yes."

Groaning with delight, he kissed her, the longest, tenderest kiss she'd ever experienced. When he lifted his face from hers, he said, "I'm going to protect you from the likes of Alvin Ashcroft, and even though the danger of the curse has passed, you still need someone to protect you."

"Thank you. I love you so much, Richard."

In the distance they could hear a faint applause from their friends.